VIRGIN
with
CHILD

Tom McDonough

The Viking Press   New York

Copyright © 1981 by Tom McDonough
All rights reserved
First published in 1981 by The Viking Press
625 Madison Avenue, New York, N.Y. 10022
Published simultaneously in Canada by
Penguin Books Canada Limited

LIBRARY OF CONGRESS CATALOGING IN PUBLICATION DATA
McDonough, Tom.
Virgin with child.
I. Title.
PS3563.A29146V5   813'.54   80-54083
ISBN 0-670-74721-1

Grateful acknowledgment
is made to Miller Music Corporation
for permission to reprint portions of lyrics
from "Ruby" by Mitchell Parish and Heinz Roemheld.
Copyright © 1953 by Miller Music Corporation.
All rights reserved. Used by permission.

Printed in the United States of America
Set in Century Schoolbook

For Mirra,
who taught me how to talk

Picture a vast plain around Jerusalem . . .
    —Ignatius Loyola,
    Spiritual Exercises

VIRGIN with CHILD

One

"Too strong for life, it seems, the Rajasthan sun," Father Sullivan said.

The temperature on the hill overlooking his mission was a hundred and thirty-nine degrees. Sullivan, his face fluorescent with sun and fourteen waxy Indian beers, was playing through his forty-third hole of miniature golf on a course of his own contrivance. He was talking to himself, his only twin.

"The Bikaner golf course, without grass, without the wind to lift a wisp of dust, dares not rise against the sky, haven't you noticed, hugs the earth in mortal submission. . . ."

His putter scuffed the ball, tacky and swollen with the heat. "Don't we all?" he replied. "Don't we all?"

His skin had transpired too much water and salt for him to sweat or even weep. He tried singing:

"Happy birthday to you, happy birthday to you . . ." Tomorrow, if he made it, he'd be thirty-seven. Only thirty-seven.

Up to a hundred and twenty or so, the heat was

merely hot. Now it was an hallucinogenic weight and the dust was a wet animal in his mouth.

He made promises to his feet, where he knew hookworms were entering through thorncuts: the minute the Cardinal dies or relents, as soon as the arguments about this exile cool off or become an embarrassment, they'll send us home, I'll make it all up to you. You'll stand in the ice-white water of that river near Woodstock, me with a rainbow on the line and you in your air-conditioned waders just like on the cover of *Field & Stream* and you'll be smelling chilly pines and you will never, never have to be this hot again, I swear.

But the sun.

His memories were a promise too. He recalled Brooklyn: himself on top of a ladder painting the flagpole while the janitor, a semi-retired Harp with a cantilevered belly, mowed the churchyard in whorls.

But the sun.

"But these villagers," he continued, "the cattle, these children without the will to brush flies from their eyes—all of them clinging to this starving mother, starving. . . ."

"Don't we all?" He sighed, scoring his eleventh consecutive hole-in-one. "Don't we all?"

At twilight, their jewelry tinkling invisibly, the full moon low in the east, women from the adjacent village filed over the embankment to the mission's holding tank and filled their jugs, stepping down into the water that trembled like something come to life after cowering all day long in the heat.

Father Sullivan was reading a recent *Batman* in his room, the dust talcuming each page by the time he turned it. It was not possible to tell if the overhead fan was pushing the adhesive air or being pushed by it. The blades wobbled, never as fast as a true spin. Sullivan slid out of his hammock and planted himself in the cushionless wicker chair that creaked every time he inhaled. He was able, after eight months at the mission, to ignore the effort it took to draw breath in these dust-oven days before monsoon.

The mosquitoes sailed in gracefully, just passing through. They didn't seem to alter their course when he struck at them. He watched them whine into the background, then managed at last to smack one between his palms. As he killed them—he couldn't miss now—he prayed for the grace to stop smoking.

The small boy who'd been haunting the garbage asked, in Bengali, for golf balls. "Bakshish, sa'ab? Timu kalagulo khete diecho ki? Bakshish?"

"Oh, bakshish yourself, Binu," Sullivan said. "Give me a break, will you?"

A few nights earlier, Binu had hit on Father O'Kane, visiting from Jaipur, for *bakshish:* for something, for anything. O'Kane had given him the silent treatment. In these matters, O'Kane, a graduate of the Pat O'Brien School of Sentimental Authoritarianism and a veteran of the subcontinent's missions, saw straight through Sullivan's objections. "Eyes front, young fellow," he had cautioned. "Give up the desire to have children."

"Bakshish?" Binu insisted. "Bakshish? Bakshish?"

Sullivan lit a Camel, took one drag and handed it to the boy, who puffed eagerly.

"All I did was write a book, Binu. Some poems. A demonstration or two . . ."

Only thirty-seven. Lately, though, he'd been dreaming of himself as an aged immigrant, cardiac and confused, assisting his grandson at the cash register of a saloon somewhere across another ocean.

Binu stared for several minutes, then left, grinning, cigarette chugging, his white shirt and trousers fading rapidly, followed by the brilliant orange scarf at his neck, its embroidered brightness eternally visible as he strolled off whistling into the *palu* trees and the wind of the nightblue palms.

"These lizards, when properly cooked, yield a white meat which is prized by those whose stomachs soar above all prejudices."

Father Sullivan's joke was intended to amuse Colonel Sethi and the two Bengali journalists, twin brothers with synchronous yawns. "Denk you, sair," they chorused when he poured their beer.

Also having dinner at the mission rectory were Natalie and Freddy Powers, the rich Peace Corps couple who loved to talk about Fellini, Cassavetes and the *Nouvelle Vague.* Sullivan was polite about Bergman's films, whose Lutheran clarity he secretly loathed. He liked *La Strada* and *Shane,* that was about it.

"What's that you're nibbling?" Natalie Powers asked. "More of those nuts again?"

"No," Sullivan said. "Pumpkin seeds, unshelled."

"Mmm," Natalie sighed expertly. "They're an acquired taste in that form."

Natalie had appeared once, for a lark, on the cover of a Mantovani album. She was French by birth, inadvertently Jewish and aristocratically negligent about her eyebrows. Sullivan had never taken much of an interest in Irish girls; he preferred to be a mystery to someone. He had prepared for this occasion by polishing off the last of Father O'Kane's Canadian Club.

Natalie's hair looked even more red this evening, luminous with a light from above, a golden ray that favored her like a loyal spotlight. The album cover, a virgin copy of which Freddy Powers kept under the front seat of his Land Rover, displayed her face in the foreground, a dim Castilian bar scene behind. She was sipping a highball and looking up. Women look up when they sip, men look down. One often thought of women as ornaments, seldom of men. Unless they were priests.

Natalie rejected the ladderback chair and helped herself to the armless rocker from Sullivan's study. Freddy sat across from her without removing the brace of Leicas around his neck.

The journalists gossiped incessantly about their exposés. Every now and then, Freddy, who was Kennedy-ized, kidded them about a particularly tall story, so everybody felt inside. Of course, the eternal day of the Rajasthan desert, the truths of people and things, retreated before their chatter, evaporating with a frightened hiss completely devoid of respect.

The colonel ate and spoke methodically, expounding on his fascination for old battlefields, sectioning his chicken like military nouns. He moved on to his experiences in air travel, which he narrated in a jaded voice, though clearly it was a novelty for him.

"As a guest of the West German government, it is like a seventh heaven. As a guest of the French government, I must ask for everything. They give it to you, but you must ask. I don't like Pan Am. Why not? This is a very difficult question."

Freddy nodded earnestly, clicking his head, a third

Leica. This morning, not being attentive to the ways of
Rajput carpentry, he had received an enlarging easel
too big to fit through his door.

One of the journalists started up, lolling and slurring
his words as if being petted.

"I love Lufthansa. On the flight they give you Polar-
ized photographs. My bag was so full. When I got to
London, they offered to arrange my accommodations. I
say: There are so many Bengalis here, sa'ab. When can
we pick you up this afternoon for the tour? they say.
There are so many Bengali friends, sa'ab. They will
show me around. They will show me all what you have
exploited from my country."

He finished on a rising note that ascended into a
giggle.

"On filth," Natalie said, skulling Freddy with a salad
pea. She gulped her beer and blew the bangs off her
forehead. This meant, approximately, that she was
angry and bored. "On filth. You ought to do one on filth.
One of your photo essays. Maybe a film, even."

Her caramel eyes were crossed at birth and the cor-
rective surgery hadn't been wholly successful. When
she laughed, she tossed her head back to disguise the
wild displacement of her pupils. One was innocent, the
other sad.

The colonel blotted his mustache on his sleeve and
said filth, yes. Word was filtering back to the canton-
ment about a villager whose head had been crushed
under the flywheel of an irrigation pump because he
misappropriated a backhoe. Natalie described a beggar
girl she'd seen near the train station. The twin journalists turned to her, offering smiles of amusement and
sympathy. Sullivan was rapt.

"Someone takes the money out of her pockets," she

said. "Someone washes her. Someone puts on her sandals. And someone cut off her arms."

She leaned forward and exhibited a burn scar the
size of a saucer on her forearm. She was famous for her
honesty.

Freddy twitched, the slave of a sudden disgust. He
cocked one of his Leicas.

"No, no," Natalie said. "No pictures now."

"It's the pose reflex," Sullivan said brightly. "Natalie
never knows whether to feel beautiful or ashamed."

Last week, when they'd all been guests at a Jain
wedding and Natalie was having her fingers painted
with hot vegetable dyes, she refused to pose for a picture with Sullivan until he mastered Bengali.

"We are not tourists," she said. "We'll have plenty of
time for that on the trip tomorrow. And will you please
stop calling me Natch?"

She concentrated on her hair, her coffee, her hands.
She knew exactly when Sullivan looked at her; her
eyes loosened. She smiled finally, lips pressed, as
though beyond them lay a secret for accidental discov-
ery.

Polite sweat leaked from Freddy's hairline. "Well, no
more talk of atrocities then, either." He lit a Gitane
and chuckled. "The wretched of this earth are especially vivid in the eyes of idealists. But surely everyone
at this table has ten fingers and an equal number of
toes."

The journalist who'd let his brother do most of the
talking, the amused one, made a rude noise and slowly
raised his left hand, grinning between his missing
fingers.

Natalie walked out and left the chair rocking behind
her.

After guava shells in cream, a special treat courtesy of the colonel, and after planning a photo expedition to the lake castle of Udaipur with Natalie and Freddy, Father Sullivan lay in bed studying the night sky through the screen, where a luna moth with a wing-span wide as his palm was thumping himself to death, the future trying awkwardly to happen. Natalie and Freddy were sleeping over in the next room. Outside, the purring of froggy bells and the plupping of water: peepers were breeding in the tank. The future was always Eve.

To take his mind off Natalie, Sullivan plotted, then solved, in the manner of a child counting backwards, the simple animal murders of the farmers he'd been assigned to save. For the hundredth time he faced his vision of the headless farmer and the armless beggar girl. Farmer, *kumar.* He was going to have to be more systematic about his Bengali. *Jelera nodir bake mach dhore binu?* Have you given Binu the bananas to eat?

Natalie's laughter came clearly through the wall. Of her words, only pitch and rhythm survived.

Sullivan fell asleep. Natalie offers him a job taking pictures for a hundred dollars an hour. No, he says, you must mean a hundred bucks a week. No, she says, a hundred dollars an hour. But that's a thousand bucks for a ten-hour day, he says. I mean what I say, she says, becoming Cardinal Spellman and speaking, like his Eminence, with a speed alarming in one so small and still. "Why do you suppose we're in Vietnam, Father Sullivan?" the Cardinal chirps. "I don't know, your Eminence," Sullivan says. "I don't know either, Father. Go away. Get lost. Take a hike."

He woke up feeling ecstatic but vaguely unsafe. He turned down the lamp. The moth tumbled from the screen and the stars came into focus. Desert stars did not twinkle like stars in crisp northern latitudes. Instead—in their oceanic leisure, high over the sands—they winked, blinked, winked. Moths looked to the stars for miracles, men for accidents they could understand and manipulate. Sullivan was superstitious about Natalie.

Thuds and flashes in the darkness. The railway workers, still on strike, were sabotaging the power plant again. A clock ticked. Insects scurried. Dust puffed through the window frames. Where *was* he? Rajasthan, yes. Sullivan meditated on the Lord Jim aspects of his missionary exile: was he just another white man with a migratory conscience? No, not everybody gets kicked by his Cardinal halfway around the world to reform unmanageable politics; not everybody's still, at his age, "a poet of promise," and not everybody's a priest. But everybody reads the funnies, he believed, and everybody sweats. This hell was not hot, it was not cold. There was only one man in hell and he was an incredibly athletic insect: see how many times his own guilt the ant can carry.

Freddy and Natalie were at it again, cooing and thrashing beyond the wall. On Sullivan's side, a beetle folded its wings like one of those planes on an old aircraft carrier. Freddy said photography was an art, a language. Sullivan knew it was nothing but a sport. Professional photography—the actual doing of it—was only a stunt, a somersault off a diving board. Sure, it took physical strength and courage, a talent for anticipation, a streak of exhibitionism, balance, practice, timing, lots of money, respect for the present and precise attention to souls just beneath the surface. But many of these things a good missionary had. That— and a secret desire to die among strangers. And some- times charm, though usually, among these Tribals, nerve would do. Sullivan knew he could take the truest picture of Natalie. He could still see her standing in the doorway, heels together to identify herself as one who has truly danced, shedding some of her glamorous glow around these clay-stark rooms.

The beetle tractored away decisively. The Cardinal in his dim executive way was providentially astute: before India, Sullivan knew nothing of hearts and en- vies. Now, he couldn't help hearing his own heart as well as Natalie's, and the sound also, he imagined, of teeth on the boards of the windows. *He* was the starv- ing farmer; *he* was the armless boy, *he* hungered, *he* thirsted. And for the first time he relished the taste of it.

Father Sullivan had no recollection of the actual impact.

At noon the next day, in sight of the crumbling tow- ers of Purana Ghat, the horizon red with dust storms from the west, just as Freddy was trying to get in a word about his collection of commemorative coins and Sullivan was listening to Natalie's remarks about the depradations of Babar, the Moghul lord who never smiled, something told Sullivan to take his eyes from the plume of golden dust choiring behind them and pay attention to the Leyland tank truck skidding across the road. All he had time to understand was that he was going to get hurt. Whunk.

What he perceived was a profound shudder, the wet dog of his existence slowly shaking himself dry. Then came the skid—a low, hysterical scraping—and the gasps and clangs and growls of strong pieces of metal suddenly changing shape.

Sullivan saw a baseball in midair, spinning in ultra-slow motion, accompanied by the hiss a professionally pitched ball makes sailing toward the plate. The ball was revolving so slowly he could count the stitches on its side. The stitches unraveled and the hide opened up and he saw the coarse string winding inside. Strand by strand the string unwound until all that was left was the black rubber core, still turning, still hissing, and as soon as this was exposed the ball began to rewrap itself and when the final stitch fell into place, the ball resumed its natural speed, breaking down and away like a perfect roundhouse curve into the catcher's mitt which had been waiting for it without a hand, and together they swooped off into dark green space.

Sullivan, searching for the baseball, noticed he was unable to account for all the parts of his body. And then it came to him that the pain which seemed to be happening everywhere was happening in his right leg and he was terrified because this pain had no limit, no name. The mashing of bone and tissue in his leg had set the pain free and it howled ingeniously, imperiously through nerves he'd never known.

He saw something close-up in his field of vision, blurry at first. He was looking at the windshield, shattered in a spiderweb pattern, blood bright at the center, his blood. He screamed. The Land Rover had been rearranged beyond recognition. Kept screaming. He tried to sort things out, but his mind stopped short of the conclusions it had to draw from the disarray of bodies, steel and blood. He heard moans. He scratched glass splinters from his scalp and cheek. Now it was quiet. A distant tinkling hum, that was all. Then, because he understood the scream was organizing his pain, he screamed again.

TWO

He used to be a lot better driver before he had his accident. He was a much better driver before his accident. He was much better as a driver before the accident happened, before the crash. He wasn't as good a driver now as he was before the accident. He didn't have as much confidence. He wasn't as confident. He went for the brakes too soon, jumped on them. He used to like to drive. Now he didn't like to drive. Because he saw possible danger too late. He was slow. He was slower. He was not as quick as he used to be. It kept occurring to him that he might have died. It kept occurring to him that he *could* die, kept occurring to him.

Father Sullivan tugged at his prick and tried to relax. He was back in darkest Brooklyn; the bar was called the Casablanca Inn. The men's room was stifling, the radiator spit on his cast, and the beers he'd been drinking since ten in the morning knifed his bladder. Because he'd fractured his skull and his right ankle, he'd made a number of adjustments large and small: he mapped each excursion according to how many steps there'd be to climb; he continued to be puzzled by the peculiar sensations in his ankle, more like a plant pushing through the soil than human pain, and he was still not used to holding his prick in his left hand while supporting himself with the aluminum cane in the right.

Sullivan held his breath, swallowed the stench and swayed beneath the bulb that illuminated beads of plumbing sweat. He read the wall from bottom to top. Three woodknots were linked obscenely. The graffiti were pretty high-strung:

Hey, Europe, eat my Florida!

Sullivan, bracing his cane in a spot where the tiles had lifted away, was inspired to add:

As a final gesture of defiance,
My uncle left his cock to science.

He'd been unable to urinate for three days after they pried him out of the Powers' Land Rover. "Neurasthenic shock," Dr. Singh had advised with a smile that was perhaps too reassuring. Finally, despite the risk of infection—the Bombay hospital floors were as foul as this men's room—they catheterized him without anesthesia, on the assumption that Americans, something like fish, did not experience pain. Miss Shrivastara, the Goanese Catholic nurse, tickled his ear with the feather of a crow who'd been shelling a cockroach enormous enough to be mourned as a pet and made him a present of extra morphine.

He spent a month in the ward with seven merchant seamen, all of them English-speaking except for Sinbad the Fly Swatter, an Ethiopian Muslim who had some Italian. Sinbad, whose real name was Rajeef, had crushed his hand under a hatch. To his cast he'd taped a flyswatter, which came to be regarded as a staff of authority around the ward. The hospital faced the Bombay shoreline, and Sullivan took to sunning himself on the balcony, often in the company of Sinbad, who'd bring his prayer rug and try to converse in Italian. Sullivan recited Virgil; they exchanged the odd *che bella figura* regarding Miss Shrivastara; they staged Frisbee tournaments with stale toast. The last three days of his stay, Sullivan took his turn as custodian of the flyswatter.

There was a stopover in Zurich, that perfect plastic flower of a town. At the Swissair counter, another missionary, returning after twenty years in Bangladesh to bury his mother, offered to pay his airport tax. Sullivan, obscurely embarrassed, declined.

"SRO in the men's room today, hah?" a voice behind him boomed. Sullivan tried to focus. He coaxed his prick. It began to dribble.

"Yessir, laze 'n' jemmin," the voice insisted. "It's SRO today. Completely, totally SRO."

The spoken word in the men's room. Very powerful. The most powerful pulpit.

The voice unzipped its fly and hosed down the sink inches from Sullivan's elbow. Sullivan's immediate reaction was to say excuse me, because clearly the voice actually lived here: this was its home and it was simply doing as it pleased.

"SRO." The man attached to the voice wore a baggy three-piece suit and smiled inanely, most likely a schoolteacher astray in his weedy eccentricities. "SRO. That's a show-business expression. It means standing room only in the men's room. How do you like this weather?"

"Well, I'll tell you something." Sullivan finally had a good flow going. "Once you've seen the vast wastelands of this world—the actual deserts, I'm talking about—you understand automatically how great religions get started in places like that. You just look at them and you can hear the hoarse, collective sigh rising: More, give us more; there has got to be more to it than this. . . ."

"Yeah, some weather," the man said. "You in show business?"

Sullivan sighed. The whooshing and plopping evoked rain on tropical leaves. Morphine. Aaah. Morphine goeth before the fall

The three-piece suit started to sing, his bray just about drowned out by the horse-cock splashing of his piss:

> They say, Ruby, you're like a song;
> You just don't know right from wrong . . .

He staggered away, a paper cocktail napkin stuck to his shoe. At the door he turned.

"Thank you, laze 'n' jemmin. Thank you, thank you. Ray Charles, laze 'n' jemmin. The genius of Ray Charles. Have moicy, have moicy. Thank you, laze 'n' jemmin, thank you, thank you, thank you. Have moicy. Thank you."

Another voice from the bar outside called, ". . . double pneumonia if you don't watch out . . ." and the door slapped shut.

Sullivan flushed the urinal.

Love is . . . What was it? He had written three vil-
lanelles, the rhythms a little rusty and hippity-hop,
about the peacocks that used to strut along the Jaipur
road in the hours of low sun, when a Land Rover could
make the drive without boiling over. Peacocks and Natalie, the only lovable things about the desert. They
were very beautiful, lazejemmin, very, very beautiful.
So many eyes in their tail fans. Everything else was an
unfaceable, faceless kind of force.

Love is . . . Let's see, the line came to him while he
was taking a leak, holding his cock in an unfamiliar
hand, so maybe . . . No, he'd lost it in the flush.

His cigarette revolved stubbornly in the urinal. He
flushed again; the blue deodorant ice cubes sizzled.

He wiped the sweat off his palms where the cane kept
digging in, crossed himself and limped in the direction
of the bar. There was a stolen rapture in the motion a
cane gave, a series of little flights. Just a second ago, he
understood this whole business. Now he was falling
asleep.

One more drink, Sullivan said to himself, and another villanelle, please, for my friend Natalie here.
Have moicy, lazejemmin, have moicy.

Somewhere, he smelled lemons. But where was her
light?

Love is . . .

"Love is a comfort when work is done," Marian's
father says the Tuesday before he dies. This is in California on their artichoke farm. It is a tired thing to say.
She is sixteen and her father is the last tired man she
wants to love. She runs away from home, assuming

that interesting things will happen to her. The first city she sees is San Francisco. Kevin, the young Jesuit with beautiful arms, invites her to go to Rome and to bed with him. She returns to the artichokes and thinks about it. A month later she is accepted into the novitiate of the Sisters of the Blessed Heart.

Sister Marian flapped the pillowcase over her head. The sound it made was exactly *plymouth.*

As a teacher of third, fifth, seventh and eighth grade kids who, if they read at all, read only comic books, she was always on the lookout for new sound effects. She was remaking her bed for the fourth time because whenever she was about to set foot outside the convent —the instant she left these rooms full of colored glass and rights and wrongs—she felt caught. Stella Maris was perhaps the tidiest parish in all of Brooklyn.

Sister Marian made a list. Brown shoes, brown belt, keys, four dimes for phone calls if needed, two subway tokens, Dr. Jimmy's phone number in case she got lost or delayed, a comb, tissues and something to read: last year's Burpee catalog with the brilliant hybrid marigolds on the back cover. Mary's-gold, whiter every year, though still more yellow than white. The Burpee people said they would pay $20,000 for the seeds of the first marigold to be judged "truly white." If Marian were still in California and if she weren't teaching thirty-seven hours a week plus preparation, that was something she'd have a crack at, breeding the perfect marigold. Something simple was all she wanted: a pure flower or a word like "love" with the lies peeled off.

Let's see, she had everything now. No, there was something else. There always was. But so what? Amen.

Sister Marian stepped into the hallway and carefully, carefully, carefully closed the door to her room. The new Sister Superior was a progressive, a subscriber to thoughtful periodicals, and she allowed locks, to which Sister Receptionist held the master key, on all doors. Sister Superior's personal policy was to keep her own door propped open at all times, most recently by a two-volume précis of the *Jesuit Relations,* from which she read aloud, during dinner hour, sagas of the mutilated French martyrs in New Canada.

The corridor was cut with slots of light. The tongue of Sister Marian's lock made a small sound as it slipped into its seat. The sound was exactly *buick.* Had the Blessed Virgin Mary actually conceived through her ear, as Abelard and St. Augustine assert?

On the stairs she approached old Sister Raymond Marjorie, who would understand from Sister Marian's civvies that she was on her way to see Dr. Jimmy. In recognition of the speed, frequency and accuracy of such surmises, Sister Raymond Marjorie was known as Sister Radar.

"Twenty years on the couch he spent." Sister Radar pinched Marian's arm. Marian leaned away as diplomatically as she could. "My brother Johnny I'm telling you about, Sister Marian. Twenty years on the couch he was. Oh, not a couch like the one in Dr. Jimmy's office, all leather and medical, Sister, but the pink-and-green one in my mother's living room, and in later years, I recall, the blue one, with my sister Fran waiting on him hand and foot, him resting up, he says, and gathering strength for another crack at the bar exam. Twenty years of rest he got, a regular horizontal saint that one, till he finally picks himself up and gets a job floorwalking in Macy's basement and works his way up in a year to manager of the diamond department, so if you ever hear of anyone getting married and they need a ring, Sister, tell him Sister Raymond Marjorie sent you and maybe the bum'll give you a break."

"Thank you very much, Sister," Marian said.

Sister Radar tucked her hands under her biceps and slinked around the corner. So many of the older Sisters and Fathers staggered, Marian had noticed, though she'd never seen one of them with so much as a cane, let alone a wheelchair. They simply moved along in whatever way they could, dispensing with intervening mechanisms, until they could move no more.

Sister Radar's slink suited her. After forty-odd years at the Sacred Heart Leprosarium in Ceylon, she had contracted, the story was, a rare form of tuberculosis. Her prosthetic knee joint made a popping noise with each step. It was as if, in moments of locomotion, her starchy black habit deliquesced into a sarong, to the accompaniment of a tiny drum.

Even after stepping out into the Lord's loud sunlight, Sister Marian could hear the pop-popping of Sister Radar's knee, echoing, clouding her sense of purpose, haunting her until she noticed, at the foot of the convent stoop, two second-graders, Fogarty and Frevola, poking red shovels through a hole in their snow fort.

Incredible. Snow so early. Two weeks to go before the Feast of the Immaculate Conception, two years to the day since Dallas, when our first Catholic President got his head shot into the half-dollars Marian could never bring herself to spend, November not nearly done, one o'clock in the afternoon on this damp fall day, the sky suddenly cleared.

At this hour of the afternoon at this time of the year, there were still some morning glories, puckered but alive, in the vacant lot across the street, twisting up through garbage smothered by the snow. Marian stepped around one of Frevola's ramparts.

"Sorry, Sister."

"That's okay, Albert." She smiled. That Frevola, such a brown nose.

Fogarty's rapid-fire snowballs, four out of five of them, ponked against the NO PARKING sign. Ponk, ponk, ponk.

Ponk.

The next bar was run by Matty McSomething-or-Other and his boy Pete, who was a little slow. For ten minutes Pete had been drying the same glass, a prisoner with his pet.

The bar gave the impression of a place where everything tended to ochre: teeth, hair, the clapboard ceiling, the cellophane tape supporting snapshots of Most Valuable Players, and the hairdos of the three women who were smoking cigarettes in a way that suggested they were all furious at the same thing. Father Sullivan had a hard-on, a dumb morning hard-on at four in the afternoon.

Roz rubbed her breasts against his arm. Roz was a knockout: her hair, which she stroked when she looked at him, was much younger than her face, and her face was the red-white-and-violet flag of her own private country. Her strategy so far was based on insinuations that the two of them were slightly notorious, Roz being an ex-quiz show contestant, Sullivan "some kind of pinko Padre."

"Let's go home, Padre. I'll make it dance like it's on a string."

"No thank you, Roz."

Sullivan's plate of stew had sweated a circle in the ancient wax. He craned his head toward Pete, who was still busy with his towel.

"Uh, I don't mean to lapse recklessly into candor here," Roz said. "But are you, uh, cherry, Padre?"

Sullivan signaled for a chaser. All right, sure, he was a virgin. He was not trying to prove anything technically. He was not a hobbyist in this life, not a contestant. Yeats was a virgin past thirty, and his finest poems were poems of regret. And what was Dante's scene, for crying out loud? Roz fingered the flannel of his shirt.

"That's a stunning outfit you got on there, Padre. Really. I'm not kidding."

Two or three nights ago, possibly at this very bar, he'd gotten a lumber jacket in trade for his cassock and his watch. It wasn't a bad deal. In the dark, he had admired the plaid. His wardrobe, when he wasn't wearing the simplest possible clothes, consisted of two leather jackets, some ties, a white tropical suit and a few high-energy Hawaiian shirts.

"C'mon, Padre," Roz said. "Suck it, fuck it, or pluck it, it all comes out the same." She let go of his collar. "C'mon, let's go."

Pete clinked an empty glass against Sullivan's cane by way of asking if he wanted a refill. Sullivan nodded why not.

"Hey Father," Pete said. "How'd you break your wing?"

"Car crash."

"Oh yeah? I never been in a car crash."

"Well, I tell you, it was an out-of-body experience, all right. Once you've seen the vast wastelands of this world, Peter . . ."

Through his nose, Sullivan exhaled into his drink. It rippled. He aimed his cane at two o'clock to locate his idea, then looked down at the whiskey again. There was a hair on the ice, not his. Perhaps he had created the wrong impression, during his first few snorts, by gossiping about Teilhard de Chardin—in Sullivan's opinion the only authentic optimist since Jesus—and Alec Guinness, his favorite convert.

He grabbed his chaser, gulped the last of it, tilting his glass straight up, the foam slithering down over his teeth. God help me, he thought. If only I couldn't think.

"I don't like white dogs," Marian said. "They're perverts."

She could not see Dr. Jimmy's face. Lying on the couch in his consulting room, this only their second meeting—session, appointment, hour?—she knew nothing about the protocol of psychotherapy except what she'd seen in television shows and *New Yorker* cartoons. To Dr. Jimmy she presented herself in symptoms.

"Is this the kind of talk you reserve for your psychiatrist, Sister?"

"I'm sorry, Doctor. Maybe I was being, you know, too melodramatic. I've always been that way, ever since I've known myself."

"Save it for your singing, Sister."

Marian had mentioned that singing was her hobby. Well, not singing exactly. Her singing voice had a huskiness that was, frankly, secular. She did write songs, though, like "Night Driving Blues." Marian's heart went *bing* when she heard beautiful music. No singer was truly hopeless.

She swung her feet off the couch and looked at Dr. Jimmy. She rebuked herself for ever imagining him with a beard. His hair, what was left of it, had been slicked back in a hasty job of repair. The pitch of his skin, the tired way it tented on his cheekbones, told her he was a drinker. He was, in fact, a "leading layman" in his field, highly recommended by Sister Carmela, the former Sister Superior. At their first meeting, when he said, "Yes, I think I can help you," she didn't believe him. But then, she hadn't believed herself when she first asked Sister Superior for permission to see Dr. Jimmy, and she hadn't believed Sister Superior when she said, "Of course, Sister. Would you like me to call him for you?" and she hadn't believed herself when, as she shook Dr. Jimmy's hand, she announced she'd been thinking of killing herself. She shuddered. It was incredibly pleasant living with this tingle of disbelief. Of course, there was the shame of admitting she had nothing but insanity to protect her heart.

"Where'd I leave off last week, Doctor?"

There was a dry silence.

"Well, let's see here. Yes. On the reflection that life is a misery, that we are all created in order to suffer, that we all know this and try to invent means for deceiving ourselves, that—"

"Oh yeah. Is it okay if I don't lie down, Doctor?"

"I'm not here to judge you, Sister, believe me. You're

free to do anything you like. The only thing I ask is, no hitting, please." Dr. Jimmy, excavating for the remains of a snack, bubbled his left cheek.

Marian lowered her eyes. She had, as a matter of fact, spotted some trophies and unusual stemware that looked like they could do with a little smashing.

"May I sit in the chair?"

Marian half-stood. She felt ashamed of the pleading in her eyes but she was helpless to erase it because it was all over her now like blisters and, yes, she could see now that Dr. Jimmy was exasperated. She transferred herself to the chair. Her elbows slipped off its chrome arms, caving in her breasts. Dr. Jimmy was pink, inert.

She told him about the convent, particularly the furnishings, like the lamps whose switches were so lightly sprung that the bulbs went on and off by themselves when a fist went down too hard three rooms away; she talked about her childhood and about her appreciation of the things ordinary people from the outside world—non-Catholics—could do. She talked about how at the age of ten, encouraged by her father, a man always enthusiastic about innovations, she devised a way to open and close the garage door without getting out of bed; she told of how, when her sixty-pound blob of papier-mâché could not be budged from the kitchen table, her mother, usually invisible amid her sewing, threatened to commit suicide. And her father called all their chickens Marian too, because chickens were too stupid to have separate names. Still, it was a home where the nights were safe.

Through all of this she sounded very strict with herself, and she wondered why, and she wondered about piercing her ears. And she thought of a thousand other sadnesses, stored since she was five.

"Am I a sad person, Doctor?"

"The Irish are sad people, Sister." Undoubtedly, Dr. Jimmy knew that Marian saw through him, as did all the priests and nuns who made up the bulk of his private practice. She knew that despite his Yale degree and his research grant at Columbia, he would always and only be a Mick and that was why he drank and that was why he wanted her, partly for revenge and partly for love, to discover this sort of thing about herself. She already knew, of course. That was her problem.

"Don't you ever dream, Sister?"

"I had relations with my brother."

"Yes. When?"

"For a long time. Then I went away to school."

"So you were in your early teens."

"No, I was three, three and a half."

"Oh, you mean before you went to *elementary* school. What kind of relations?"

"I don't really remember. He told me later, sexual relations. . . ."

"And that would make your brother, let's see, about five or six at the time." Dr. Jimmy sniffled axiomatically.

Marian wasn't sure how old Brian would have been. She was no longer sure where she was. She tightened her grip on the chair and tried to put away the thought she might be in China or Ohio. She searched for something to say.

The silence was perforated by a light crackling: Dr. Jimmy appeared to be unwrapping a small package in his lap.

"It's my lunch," he said without looking up. "Excuse me, I'm starving." He put his mouth around the BLT on toast. "It's my lunch hour," he said, pointing at something. His wrist. But there was no watch on it.

Marian pointed sympathetically at her own wrist,
though it, too, was watchless.

"Where was I?" she said.

"I don't know, Sister." Dr. Jimmy peered over his
BLT, then lowered it. His thumb seemed to be in an odd
place: between the lettuce and toast. Oh, it was not his
thumb, of course. It was his penis, a real zucchini, poking through the abundant sandwich.

Marian sobbed. Dr. Jimmy raised the sandwich; that
provoked another gush of tears. She groped in her
purse but couldn't locate her tissues. She discovered
instead her rosary, which she hadn't intended to bring.
Silently she begged the pardon of birds made homeless,
or turtles unshelled. She feared his penis as one fears
animals in a dream. Silence coated her.

"Why am I crying, Doctor?"

"I don't know, Sister." His face had relaxed into the
incomparably sweet look of an old man listening to an
old song.

"Body language is our first language," she'd read just
the other day in *Commonweal.* "Norman O. Brown and
the New Paganism," the article was called. It was by
a Benedictine with a German name. And what was Dr.
Jimmy's sandwich saying except: Relax, Sister, relax.

She said nothing for the remaining five minutes of
her hour. Dr. Jimmy did not disturb his BLT.

Finally, glancing again at her empty wrist, Sister
Marian stood up, and Dr. Jimmy did the same. She
walked toward the door, listing away from him, as
she'd done with Sister Radar on the stairs.

"Tell me, Sister, are you familiar with the Irish joke
about the Irish mother who cut out her Irish heart and
gave it to her Irish daughter to give to her Irish boy-
friend?"

"No, Doctor. I can't remember jokes."

"Well, of course you can't. There's no such joke." Dr. Jimmy zipped up and slapped her playfully on the cheek. "Cheer up, Sister. Pull yourself together. What kind of gum is that you're chewing?"

"Dentyne, Doctor. Would you like a piece?"

"It has a funny smell." Dr. Jimmy wiggled his nose, but the effect was false.

Marian smiled. She chewed harder, swallowed a trickling swallow. Louder than a brook, it seemed.

And yes, she thought, I know where I am.

She tipped the bottle of Robitussin from his desk into her purse.

Swallowing, louder than a brook: my body is my address.

"Negs war weather dishes," Sullivan said.

Outside this bar there were six baby carriages and two grandmothers. Inside was full of people who had survived several styles of popular music and still insisted on Vic and Bing. The jukebox crooned.

Sullivan shook his head and tried to clear his eyes. "Negs war weather dishes."

The Swede was a great audience. He understood very little but he kept laughing, which made Sullivan think: Here's a guy with a decent sense of humor. Until he remembered he wasn't trying to be funny. The Swede was featureless, the way Swedes are, except for his nose, a great old purple boot of a thing, pebbly and disorderly.

"Negs war weather dishes," Sullivan said gravely, tucking in his chin. "Negs war . . . the negs war . . . will be fought . . . the next war will be fought under weather dishes . . . fought under 'streme weather conditions. Conditions. Extreme weather conditions."

Someone stepped on Sullivan's foot. It was a skinny kid carrying a beer pail. He had a face like a cartoon: curly red hair parted down the middle and a map full of freckles, serious as a prelapsarian shortstop. Roz, still along for the ride, hoisted the kid on the bar.

"Give him a drink, Dermot," Sullivan said, suddenly realizing this wasn't the next bar. This was where he'd started out this morning. It was just that the bartender had put on his blaze-orange vest while reciting a bow-hunting story—that threw him off a little. Okay, well a frog only sees what he can eat.

"Sure," Dermot said. "You been to Mass yet, kid? What'll it be?"

The kid opened his mouth and worked his jaws, uttering a soft squawk, incomprehensible but somehow precise. The last prism of Sullivan's sobriety told him the kid could not possibly have said "Uruguay."

"You got it, Peanuts," Dermot said. He swung a highball glass under the ginger ale tap and topped it off. He cuffed the kid behind the ear with the flat of his hand. The kid's curls took a little hop. He jumped off the bar. Sullivan winked at Dermot and rapped the kid another one, this time on top of his head. The kid clonked Sullivan on the shin. Sullivan laughed once, explosively, then turned back to the Swede.

"So listen, squarehead. D'ja ever hear the one about the talking dog who knew all about our national pastime?"

The Swede blinked amiably. Sullivan felt the time was right for a canine joke: this was a neighborhood where people were proud of the tricks their dogs could do. He draped an arm over the kid's shoulders.

"Whyncha give the kid a snort, Dermot?"

"He already did, Padre." Roz flicked her boa in private celebration of something. "Steady, now."

"Okay, great, Roz, great. Okay, so this one guy says to the other guy, How much you wanna bet this dog of mine knows everything about baseball, and the other guy says, Okay, and the first guy says, Gowon, Fido, tell my friend here who hit the most home runs in one season and the dog goes Woof!"

The jukebox was between numbers. The loudest noise suddenly was the tinkle of ice cubes in the kid's ginger ale.

"Woof!" Sullivan barked. "Woof! Rooth! Get it? Woof! Rooth—Babe Ruth! The dog goes Woof! See?"

Sullivan poked the Swede in the chest. The Swede rolled with it, not laughing. Sullivan poked him again, and again the Swede rolled with it. His hands were stuffed in his pockets.

"Woof!" Sullivan barked.

The Swede's fist jumped out of his pocket. It was wrapped around a roll of quarters. The roll shattered when it crashed into Sullivan's jaw. While he was arriving on the floor, hands slamming into the boards just ahead of his face, Sullivan listened to the quarters jingle. He rolled back on his knees and groped for the side of his head, missing. Blood spurted between his fingers. He tried to spit, but his mouth was so numb that all he did was spray more blood across his lips and chin.

"Woof!" the Swede barked.

Sullivan's arms dangled forward, slightly out of plumb. He sniffed the sourness, not quite committed to staying upright, just thinking about it, ready to forget it, out on his feet, the taste of ripped flesh stale and metallic on his tongue. He staggered toward the Swede and raised his hands, palms out. Nothing there. The

Swede smiled, checked his flanks and stepped backward to the door.

"Well, so much for Mr. Integrity," Roz remarked. "And him the great pacifist."

Sullivan asked Dermot for a napkin to wrap his teeth in. He spit three more teeth, trailing blood and beer, into the sink. The speechless Uruguay kid, his freckles two shades paler, stared at him. Sullivan smiled, suddenly sober. He was a priest again. Men who are called Father, he remembered, liked to mother little boys.

"You okay, Padre?" Roz inquired.

The flash of a passing windshield blinded him. He was suddenly on one knee.

"I'm swell, thanks, Roz. All I need's a beer and an ashtray and I'm all set."

Sister Marian removed her mittens, unwrapped another stick of Dentyne, plaster-stiff from the cold, and began to chew it, forgetting everything, forgetting Dr. Jimmy.

The subway strap had somebody else's gum on it; she grabbed the pole and stood looking upriver while the train clanked across the bridge, girders and signposts retreating in dizzying streaks. The sun came out again, gilding plump snow clouds. Below, the river itself had become a source of light. A tugboat poked a barge against the current: intersecting wakes quilted the water. A McGillicuddy tug it was: the *Sheila*, christened by Michael J. McGillicuddy, a flashy Holy Cross quarterback, class of '39, in honor of his wife these twenty-odd years, also flashy. The McGillicuddys were nice boys from Park Slope who named all their tugs after McGillicuddy wives and mothers. The Morans, their great rivals, did the same.

The sun trickled down Marian's neck in time to the clacking of the expansion joints ... because ... because, across the aisle, the tips of a baby's fingers were trembling because the train was trembling because in this tremble was the tremble of the entire mortal world yearning for . . .

No.

Sister Marian sat down, the light still rolling on the river. She was twenty-six. She was young and she was Irish, but she was not so young and Irish that love, or thoughts of love, could kidnap her completely.

At the other end of the car, a teenage girl, a Puerto Rican girl—blossomy lips, heavy eyebrows, earrings lower than her hair—was looking at the ceiling and yawning with her jaws only, mouth locked. She crossed her legs. Marian crossed hers. There were nicks on them, little dents, and stubble like a rash. All summer long, right into October, she'd sunned herself on the fire escape, and as soon as the weather warmed up, she'd get out there again. She was wearing a plaid skirt that was either *supposed* to be too long or just *happened* to be too long; she wasn't an expert on such things. The train rumbled into the tunnel. She sucked her fingertips and reviewed the times she'd been lucky: finding that five-dollar bill and the Patek Philippe watch on the street in Boston all in one week. But she lost things too, and she often smelled of toothpaste.

Three boys hung over her, looking at the route map. The lights went out.

"Fuckin' Lindsay!" the tall one said. Melting snowflakes sparkled in his mustache. She was surrounded by Africans.

Lord, let me take another train.

At Fifty-ninth Street she changed for the local. On one of the columns, in a carefully sketched heart, someone had scribbled: *Cisco & Mona, lovers to the bone, 3/17/65. Happy St. Paddy's Day.*

She decided to call the convent and let them know she'd be a few minutes late. She found one of her dimes and dialed the phone under Cisco & Mona's valentine.

"Hello, St. Mary's Star of the Sea Rectory and Convent. Speak when you hear the beep. God loves you." Then came Sister Receptionist's voice, live, on top of the answering machine. Once again, she'd forgotten how to turn it off. "Stella Maris, hello? Stella Maris, hello?"

Another express screeched into the station and Sister Marian was unable to hear her own voice. She shouted into the phone, biting each syllable out of the air:

"This is Sister Lucky. Luh-KEY. El-You-See-Kay-Why. Sister Lucky. See you later."

Father Sullivan propped himself up diagonally in the phone booth. Peanuts, the kid, waited outside, scanning a *Spiderman* and pretending not to know him, but keeping close. Roz said, "Yoo hoo, Padre—bye-bye," and flapped her boa sarcastically. She couldn't hear what Sullivan was saying, but she saw him dialing numbers and dropping dimes.

He dialed Dr. Silberman. He tried him again at home. Of course. It was Saturday.

"Howdy," Silberman said.

Sullivan explained his teeth. "This is not Vietnam, Monroe, but it's important."

"Well, it's important to you, maybe. Me, I just got back from Miami, I don't even know my own name. Besides, it's my day off and I got a rehearsal with the quartet any minute."

Sullivan's knee crumpled. He'd known Silberman for ten years; he'd never asked him what quartet or why he often referred to himself as "the raincoat of the Communist Party in Brooklyn, USA." What Sullivan did know, from bumping into him at the Spartacists' League, was that Silberman's wife, after forty-three years, had just divorced him. He mourned her: "She swam laps like a motorboat; she had a recipe for lobster sauce made from tile fish." And his unwanted freedom was pinched with ironic penances: his teeth and his cruisewear were snazzy; his girlfriends all were tyrants. He was a dentist.

"Monroe, please. I don't want to go to a stranger."

"What am I, a close personal friend of your front teeth?"

"Look, I just took one on the chin, that's all."

"You people have got to learn to stop mixing intoxicants and armed struggle."

"We sure can sing and dance though."

"Come around in an hour."

Radiantly dentured, meticulously bald, a patch of pink scalp between hedges of hair, Dr. Monroe Silberman yanked the fiddle from under his chin, blew the lint out of the corduroy-lined carrying case and tucked his instrument away. He turned to Father Sullivan—Peanuts was in the waiting room rearranging Silberman's display of ceramic dogs—and stood with his finger to his lips, replaying the cadenza in his head.

"Not bad for a Trotskyite, hah?" he said.

Sullivan unwrapped his teeth. Silberman tossed them into the wastebasket, clinkclank, then prepared a novocaine. "Dee-diddle, diddle-dee-dee," he hummed. Sullivan groaned.

"I know, I know," Silberman said. "Nobody likes injections. It has to do with the fear of penetration, Freud says. You know what the Hungarians say? They say how come a man has thirty-two teeth and only one *schwanz?* I'll tell you why. So I can make a living, that's why. When I was a kid, was the Depression. Who could be a fiddle player?"

The hypodermic was suspended next to Sullivan's cheek. He sighed and kneaded his nose, trying to control his idiotic smile. Silberman waved the needle.

"So I'm not a kid anymore. The big shots, some of them from the central committee, the number one guys, they're all retired already: Florida, Miami Beach, Boca Raton, Tarpon Springs. In '47, you went to Miami for a visit, they kicked you out of the Party for white chauvinism. So now they're all after me, the number one guys, I should come down to live. Every December they call me, my pals, I should eat my heart out. You know what I tell them?"

"What do you tell them?"

"I'll tell you what I tell them: Zey alle sitzen dorten in zey varten far dem malchimuvis zol zey kimmen nemmin—az der malchimuvis vill mir dar yich nicht setzen dorten—valten fahrem—zol er kimmen kicken far mir."

Sullivan let his eyes drift through the venetian blinds, down along the shops on Third Avenue two stories below. *Cat Ballou* was still showing at Loew's Electra. Lee Marvin and Jane Fonda, their thin lips and tortured eyes incestuously matched. Last Friday afternoon he woke up in the middle of the movie.

"You know what that means?" Silberman said. "I'll tell you what it means. It means the number one guys, they're all sitting around waiting for the angel of death. But if the angel of death wants me, why should I go to him? Let the sonofabitch come and get me."

"Malchimuvis? That's the angel of death?"

"You're a smart boy." Silberman leaned forward to administer the injection.

"Haec se caminibus promittit solvere mentes," Sullivan said. "Ast aliis immitere curas, sistere aquam fluvius, et vertere sidera retro. . . ."

"What's that? What?" A faint connoisseur's smile.

"That's Virgil. Talking about the, uh, I think it must have been the Cumaean Sibyl. 'Her charms could ease your pain, fill your heart like the sail of a ship, or bring pain back again; could stall floods, could turn the stars around. . . .' "

Silberman massaged Sullivan's purple jaw to speed the anesthetic.

"People don't worry so much about sex in the Soviet Union." He started his drill. "And by the way, Jack, if you smell something burning, don't worry. It's only you."

There was blood on the chin strap of Sister Radar's crash helmet.

A woman sporting three distinct species of fur said,

"Maybe we should take it off." A whiteness, the barely discernible dust of a disaster, hung in the air.

"Maybe we shouldn't," the man kneeling next to her said. "She might've hurt her neck."

The cabdriver was still in his cab. "She shouldna been there," he said to his fare.

There by the fire hydrant was Sister Radar, her prosthetic leg jutting out at a rag-doll angle, snared in the rear fender of her motor scooter, which had been shipped all the way from Ceylon, now just a leaking pile of scrap. Sister Marian ran to her, ran past the Christmas trees trussed and orphaned in the used car lot, ran past the Cuban boys being cruel to a white cat, ran to Sister Radar, whose cape was flapping like the wing of a specimen butterfly come unpinned.

"Sister Raymond Marjorie, Sister Raymond Marjorie. Sister Raymond Marjorie!"

When the squad car pulled up, the first thing the cop did was take off Sister Radar's crash helmet. More blood gushed underneath. The cop asked Sister Radar how she felt. She squeaked feebly.

"You a friend of this individual's?" The cop was already writing something down, the report pad propped on his belly.

"I am," Sister Marian said.

"Can you give me the individual's name?"

"Yes I can, officer."

"All right. Give me her name, please."

"Sister Radar."

"Spell it, please."

"Sister Radar Marjorie. Sister *Raymond* Marjorie." Sister Marian broke into tears. "Oh Sister Raymond Marjorie, Sister Raymond Marjorie!"

"And your name, bud?"

"Sullivan," the kneeling man said.

"You got a brother in the two-oh?" the cop asked.

"Huh?"

"Billy Sullivan in the twentieth precinct—he your brother? You look like him."

"I do?"

Sister Marian became aware of the weight of Sister Radar's head, which she was sharing with the individual beside her. She didn't know why she hadn't noticed his sandals before. He wore only one sandal actually, that over a woolen sock so gaudy it might once have been a cap. His other foot was in a plaster cast. The tip of it, filthy and already shredded, was dissolving in the slush. Nothing was visible in his sunglasses but the reflection of a triangular slab of snow next to her knee. His jacket was missing some buttons. His shirttail hung below it, giving him the look of a blanketed horse. Sister Marian kept encountering this person's fingers through the wisps of Sister Radar's hair.

"Maybe we should call a doctor," he said.

"They already did," she said, nodding at the cops. The man shrugged.

"Maybe *you* should call a doctor," Marian said.

"I am a Catholic priest, miss."

Marian stopped being astonished by him. His sandals, given this awful weather, were proof of otherworldly orientation. The sunglasses, however, remained questionable.

"Well, I am a Catholic nun," Marian said.

"She *is,* Father," Sister Radar said, raising her head with a ghastly effort and giving Marian a chance to escape the man's fingers.

"Then stop behaving like a moron, Sister," he said to Marian. Then, turning to Sister Radar: "Maybe you shouldn't try to move, Sister."

"Excuse me, Father," Sister Radar moaned.

The spinning red light of the ambulance swooped across his sunglasses. He jerked upright. Marian watched him pointing with his cane, for the benefit of the ambulance attendants, to Sister Radar's leg and helmet. Let him officiate, Marian thought. Nuns knew things about the priesthood hidden from priests themselves: they were merely ticket-takers. The vestments were the show. At birth, every soul bought a ticket: the body. What more really had to be done? Marian tried to keep thinking in this vein, but she was distracted by a little wave from Sister Radar when they slid her inside.

The man stepped on Marian's toe; her nipples lit up. He hopped in the ambulance, swinging his bad leg after him. It struck Marian that his pose—arms one way, head another, intent on Sister Radar—was a sort of Pietà, only with the roles of mother and son reversed.

"I didn't catch your name, Father?" she said.

"Jack. Are you a cop, too?"

Marian could see he was embarrassed with her. He took off his sunglasses and stuffed them in his pocket without completely folding the frames. Clack. Despite deep creases of self-accommodation at the edges, his green eyes were startlingly harmless. Large, sensitive eyes; they could fool you. Eisenhower had large, sensitive eyes.

"I'm sorry for my words to you a moment ago, Sister. I've been out of the country. Also my teeth are killing me."

"It's all right, Jack."

"I know it's all right, Sister." His hand stiffened on the door. The front page of somebody's *Post* (the headline: MORE SNOW!!!) fluttered at her feet. When she looked up, the man had replaced his sunglasses.

"Where are you from, Sister?" he asked.

"California, Father."

"I mean what parish?"

"Oh. This parish, Father. Stella Maris."

"Do you like it here?"

"It's so cold." She hugged herself, chilled at the implication that she must have a choice about where she was. She felt her ears traveling around her head. "It doesn't do this in California."

"What, Sister?"

"The weather, Father. I mean, there are times when I like it. Brooklyn is so ugly, though."

"But Brooklyn must be somebody's idea of what's beautiful, Sister. Brooklyn is Paris for some people."

"Yes, Father. Well, Father, love is blind, I guess. Would you like some gum?"

"No thank you, Sister. And love is not blind. Lust is blind."

"Yes, Father."

"Love is deaf, Sister."

Just as she was about to inquire if he were a Jesuit, he shut the door, thud. The ambulance pulled away, exhaust pipes puffing in the frost. She stepped back to escape the flying slush; she stared after him like the first song she'd ever heard. A grave wind molested him; he vanished.

When Sister Marian got back to the convent, she took a long hot shower in the dark. She sat down in the tub, engulfed by clouds of blue steam.

Then she went to her room, locked the door and listened to Martha and the Vandellas, also in the dark.

Three

What Peanuts Kennedy liked most about Uruguay were his wings, of course, and the way he could soar. Whenever Sister Marian called on him, Peanuts shivered in the coolness of Uruguay's huge hovering shadow. He felt himself glide out the window and join Uruguay somewhere over the schoolyard, where the walls of the school and the church pulsed like coals with the glow from his slowly fanning wings. They'd lift away, up over the tombstone rows of tenements and semi-attached houses, vaulting the Half Moon Hotel and the parachute jump in Coney Island, and beyond the bay to the sea, the boat horns groaning and the seagulls spiraling, but never so far as to sail completely out of sight of the other fifth-graders, who were able to track them by the silver glints from Uruguay's breastplate. "Is that really Peanuts?" they murmured, bunching against the window. "Yeah, it's him, the dope. It's a miracle."

———

"Dennis?" Sister Marian was saying. "Mr. Kennedy? Are you with us today? Sometimes I wonder about you, Mr. Kennedy."

Sometimes I wonder about you, too, Sister, Peanuts commented to Uruguay. He nodded, blushing, breathless from his flight.

Sister Marian never let him drift too far away and she never called him Peanuts, the way everybody else did, just for being such an expert on comic books. It was around the time President Kennedy got shot that Peanuts began to stutter, only slightly at first, but building in clownishness and intensity till all he could say was a single word—*Uruguay*—the secret name of his special guardian. The late President was no relation. But way back, his father said, we all were kings. So who could tell?

Something tumbled from Sister Marian's coronet. A beret. She kept on calling the fifth-grade roll while fishing for it. "Maguire . . . Nolan . . . Russo . . ."

She tucked her beret in the roll book. "This morning, boys and girls, we are going to close our catechisms and we are going to play—*pay,* I mean—strict attention to our visitor."

She laughed at her mistake. Of all the nuns and priests Peanuts knew, their faces always so skeptical of a good time, lifeless and proud as outdated calendars, Sister Marian's smile—her heart, he supposed—was uniquely quick and willing. He stared grimly. His was a case of nun-worship so severe there was nothing funny about it.

As for the visiting missionary, motionless so far, lounging against Sister Marian's desk, he was looking about the same as when the Swede put him away, except now he was wearing his white tropical cassock, which seemed a couple of sizes too large. He scratched the beginnings of a beard and sagged like a glove on a stick.

There was a commotion in the vicinity of Crazy Doyle's desk: his catechism and pencil case clattered to the floor. Sister Marian clapped her hands and directed Doyle with a gun-barrel finger to stand. He slouched like a gangster, one hand hitched in his belt.

"We are going to close our catechisms *quietly,* aren't we, Mr. Doyle, and we are going to stand up straight— and I mean *straight right now*—young man, and we are going to pay strict attention or we are going to wind up cleaning erasers after school till we are blue in the face, aren't we, Mr. Doyle? Jack is expecting better behavior here in Brooklyn than in the foreign missions. I mean . . ."

Sister Marian caught her breath. The kids held theirs. She flicked a finger. Doyle sat down. Her tone turned catechetical, stiff.

"And now Father Jack Sullivan will tell us all about his missionary work in pagan lands."

From the folds of his cassock Father Sullivan pulled a switchblade knife and an orange. He tossed the orange in the air and speared it as it fell.

"Well," he said, "I'm a scrawny rascal, aren't I?"

He tucked up his cassock, a signal for the kids to feel relaxed and entertained instead of sermonized. Sister Marian began erasing the blackboard, stalled in mid-wipe, looked over her shoulder.

"Well, to tell you the truth," Father Sullivan said, shoving off from the desk, "—and that never does much harm when you're talking to kids—I don't have a whole lot to say about the missions, at least not until his Eminence says I do. In the meantime, it's all just captions in the *National Geographic.* . . ." He started skinning the orange. The blade was rusty. He let the peels fall rhythmically. "Coconuts thudded in the soft white sand. My skin was dark. My machete caught the sun, split the shell and spilled the milk. Rocking chairs rocked against a background of trinitarias. I hung whiskey corks from my hat to scare away the flies." The kids loved it. "I wore a tie and a watch. I believed in snapshots. I was a tourist. . . ."

Sister Marian scrubbed the blackboard.

"So here we are in Brooklyn, boys and girls, land of infants in uniform, as they say in the *National Geographic.*" Father Sullivan pried off a section of orange. "But let's get down to business now. I'm here to ask you what you'd like to be when you get older and it's time for you to set sail in this wide world. In other words, what is your vocation, your calling."

As usual, Margaret Mary Fatso Finnegan had her flipper in the air first. Margaret Mary knew all the answers. Peanuts didn't think his stuttering was such a terrible handicap when he looked at Fatso. Peanuts may have been strange, but he was no stranger than the Donnelly triplets, who smoked like chimneys from the age of eight, had a tideline of tar across their teeth, never wore socks and never took a bath; no stranger than Jewel Cherry Jackson, the only colored kid in Stella Maris and the only kid of any color who wasn't named after an official saint; and he was no stranger than Margaret Mary Fatso herself, with such a beautiful face and her hair a mass of naturally curly jet-black ringlets, and her two arms, not having grown at all since the day of her birth, stunted like flippers, not even able to join in the gesture of prayer. Plus she was fat.

"A saint, I'd like to be, Father," Margaret Mary said.

"That's lovely," Father Sullivan said. "A saint. A heart to change the world. And were you thinking of any kind of saint in particular with that fine curly head of yours?"

Margaret Mary nibbled a ringlet. She answered nervously and neatly, armstubs semaphoring and head cocked as if reciting from the pages of an apparitional catechism quivering six inches over her head. "A movie star, Father," she said.

"Lovely. Of course, it's not always easy to do God's work in the movies these days."

Sister Marian dropped her four-color pen and covered it with her sleeve. "Yes, Father. Margaret Mary means she'd be a saint first, Father, then a movie star."

"Lovely, Sister. And what about this young scholar?"

Crazy Doyle got up, repeating his wise-guy slouch and smoking a piece of chalk. "I'm gonna be a garbageman, Father."

Sister Marian clicked her pen, changing colors.

"Lovely," Father Sullivan said. "And why's that?"

"Well, 'cause garbagemen are a lot like missionaries, Father."

"Hmm?"

"They, y'know, travel around and see the world."

Sister Marian narrowed her eyes. Doyle smirked, ducked. Father Sullivan popped a section of orange into his mouth and hoisted a leg on Peanuts' desk.

"And what about this learned gentleman? Are you another humorist?"

Father Sullivan's smell was familiar. On his father's breath, Peanuts didn't like the smell of liquor; on the priest it was exotic, a spice. The orange dribbled.

Sister Marian stood by, tenting her hands, fingertips

touching, palms pushing apart, returning, pushing apart.

Peanuts was thinking he'd like to be a missionary priest because Crazy Doyle was right, they did get to travel around a lot, and what could be more interesting than to find out where things were? With Uruguay he'd fly away to a spicy island where he'd wear white clothes and save the pagans. He would nurse them; he would contract their diseases; he would cure them miraculously, and as he lay dying, just before he left for heaven, the colors of the sky would deepen and he would sing songs of his home to the dark pagan children with their knowing pagan eyes and their white-bellied fingers would tremble on their drumheads while he sang and they sang, and his voice, clear as the singing of the skinny saints themselves, would dance out over the waveless, God-reflecting waters.

"Uruguay," Peanuts said.

Sister Marian's fingers fell together, meshed.

Father Sullivan's expression flashed from curiosity to appraisal.

"Dennis means, Father . . ." She came closer.

Father Sullivan's hand darted to hers, then away. He turned to the whole class.

"Well, this is a very hard question, boys and girls, and you've all answered very well. If we had time this morning to go all around the room, I'm sure each and every one of you would be thinking of offering your life in some spectacular way for the glory of Almighty God."

He flipped his switchblade from one hand to the other. The knife, rather, stood still in the air while he rocked his hands back and forth, clasping and unclasping. The floating knife was his fulcrum.

Crazy Doyle, under his desk, rapidly zipped and unzipped his fly, producing a whistling noise too mysterious to be traced. Sister Marian glowered.

"So if there's any of you interested in the saving of
pagan souls . . ." Father Sullivan straightened up,
steadied himself and glanced at Sister Marian as if
remembering a cue. He resumed his speech in County
Brooklyn bel canto, a bit of the old sermonizing brogue
thrown in. ". . . if you're interested in the saving of
pagan souls, and I'm sure all of you are, you won't be
forgetting now will you to fill your mite boxes with
pennies for the foreign missions as quickly as you can,
for the doing of it will greatly increase your chances of
attaining eternal bliss in our lord Jesus Christ, and
that's eternal bliss I'm talking about, not the movies or
television, with all due respect, nor any of those plea-
surable but passing fancies like some I've lately seen."

He sagged on Peanuts' desk, revived himself with
more orange, and angled in the direction of Sister
Marian, who had returned to her desk and was busy
picking staples out of some papers.

"There's one more question I'd like to ask of you,
boys and girls, just one, and then you'll be rid of this
stranger. Here it is: what do you suppose, boys and
girls, is the one temptation, the single deadliest sin,
that the devil puts in the way of each and every one of
us and our heavenly vocation, whatever that calling
may be: sainthood, sanitary engineering or stardom on
the silver screen?" He gobbled his words with the last
of the orange. "Come on now, boys and girls. Let's give
this a little serious thought. The single deadliest sin,
let's have the answer."

Dirty Dot McDermott grinned at the ceiling. Tommy
DeFazio, Billy Ferrugia and Crazy Doyle grinned at

Dirty Dot. Peanuts' entire sex life flashed before him: underwear.

Father Sullivan wheeled around at the class. "No, no, it's not that one. Not the sin of impurity in thought or deed. This is the devil's own favorite I'm talking about now, the trickiest sin of all, and the loneliest, the sin from which all sins flow, the sin of angels as well as mortal men. Now, who has the answer?"

Peanuts knew.

But no hands went up, not even Margaret Mary Fatso Finnegan's flipper.

"What? Has Sister Marian not drilled you on this one, boys and girls? If we know our catechism the way we should, no sin can surprise us, isn't that so, Sister? No one knows?"

Father Sullivan hoisted the window pole from its socket and tucked it under his arm, the switchblade still open in his hand, sort of double-barreling it. "No one knows?"

Peanuts knew. The sin of angels and men, that was easy. He knew, he knew. Peanuts informed Uruguay that he felt like a deaf person watching people dance.

Sister Marian tucked a strand of hair under her coronet. Dirty Dot McDermott winked at Crazy Doyle. *Peanuts knew.* Sister Marian had observed last Tuesday that Miss McDermott, with all her makeup, looked like Halloween, only every day. *He knew.* Dirty Dot had replied privately that Sister Marian only said that because *she* didn't have to worry what *she* was going to wear on *her* face every day.

"No one knows?" Father Sullivan slumped on the window pole, muttering something Peanuts couldn't make out, over and over, then set the window pole against the wall and hobbled to the blackboard, where he hesitated for a second before extending his knife to Sister Marian, seemingly distracted by the top of her desk, chin braced on her wrists, a pose she suddenly broke by plunging a hand into her habit and passing a piece of chalk to Father Sullivan, who dropped the knife and gingerly took the chalk, tenderly almost, roll-ing it between his fingers slowly at first, then faster and faster, until he started to scribble on the blackboard with a force that cracked the chalk point four times, leaving him, as he finished, his lips blue and trembling, with nothing but a powdery stub, and his voice a shout on the final word:

"Lente, lente currite, noctis *equi!*"

He smashed the chalk to dust and puffed trium-phantly.

"Latin!" he said hoarsely. "Latin, boys and girls! The official language of Holy Mother Church—though Jesus himself spoke no Latin that we know of—and the language of the holy sacrifice of the Mass, the language known and loved wherever the word of Almighty God has been heard these past nineteen hundred years. Until next October, that is, when the Mass goes to English and everyone'll find out what mumbo-jumbo it really is."

Father Sullivan surveyed his scribbling, in search of a destination.

"Oh, and yes, boys and girls, let me remind you of something else, and this is no mere coincidence: Latin also happens to be the language of the greatest pagan land of them all . . ."

Peanuts knew, he knew. His knuckles were white on the sides of his desk.

". . . a land so far, far away that only a few of the bravest missionaries have seen it, and only a few of them, for the briefest of moments. It's the land, boys and girls, the land that's known . . ."

He sprinted back to the window pole, snatched it and slammed the butt against the floor.

". . . the land that's known as *epic poetry!*"

Sister Marian buried her face in her hands.

"Lente, lente currite, noctis *equi!* 'Run slowly, run slowly, run slowly, you horses of the night!' Oh, how much better Virgil's mother tongue says it for him, boys and girls. *'Slow*ly, *slow*ly, take it *slow*ly, *hors*es *run*ning in the *night!'* "

He beat out the locomotive rhythm with the butt of the window pole: crackcrack*crack,* crackcrack*crack,* crackcrack*crack.*

"Virgil," he said. "Virgil, Virgil, Virgil, Virgil! He stands there like a mountain, boys and girls. You've only to go around him. There's no going over him, not Virgil. So when you write a line like that, boys and girls, stuff it in your mite box and mail it to me. Mail it to me and die young."

Sister Marian bolted to attention, her test papers scattered.

Peanuts was on his feet too, propelled by the answer exploding in his lungs.

"P-p-pride!" he shouted.

"Or was that Ovid?" Father Sullivan mumbled, wandering toward the door. He scrubbed his mouth; chalk dust stormed from his beard.

"Pride!" Peanuts shouted.

"Oh yeah, that's right—the sin of pride. Very good, young man, very good. The sin of angels as well as mortal men. Pride and his stepbrother, jealousy." He tossed a wink at Sister Marian. "But what can you know of jealousy at your age, boys and girls? Good morning to all of you, and thank you very much, Sister."

He was gone. The glass in the door shivered behind him.

Peanuts missed him instantly. Until Father Sullivan turned up in his classroom, he'd never heard of such a thing as exile.

The bell rang. In the confusion of escape, Peanuts got the switchblade.

Four

Snow on Mount Abu, pink in its highest dawn, is more of a miracle than flight itself. On the plane no one confides in you, as travelers often do.

The Rajasthan desert, from five thousand feet, is the color of rust. The haze is not water vapor. There is no water. The haze is dust. India is dust, very old dust.

Your plane lands in Bombay at seven in the morning. The temperature is a hundred and ten. Customs confiscates your Kodak. The jitney must wait for the plane from Nepal, which arrives, astonishingly, on time, disgorging two Australian girls, a conservative-looking couple from Oregon who make jokes about rain, an English hippie, two Nepalese, one with a rose pasted on his forehead, and a retired Baptist minister doodling on his hometown newspaper. The heat accelerates. Benares, the English boy says, is too much into death, burning bodies and all that. Bright green birds chuckle.

On the way to the hotel you hang your head out of the jitney and let a hot breeze blow spittle from the side of your mouth. There is no water. There is no coolness.

Not even their memories exist. Only movie posters
with axes and purple Krishna faces. The gateway of the
Imperial Hotel is flanked by bearers who lean tensely
in your direction. "No reservations, sa'ab, sorry." You
lean against a stuccoed column, scalding your shoulder
blades. On the way up the Janpath, taxi drivers, their
eyes all mirrors, call to you. No, no, you are going to
walk it. A girl no more than ten follows you, an infant
clawing at her breast. She pokes you; you keep walking. She smiles feverishly, runs ahead, falls behind.
She rips open her blouse and says, "Nothing touch."
You are about to faint. You hallucinate a cultist with
a long curly dagger poised to mutilate your eyes and
your genitals and haul your body off somewhere and
you will be dead and that will be that and it will be a
relief. The road tilts, about to spill.

Half a mile away, the hotel shimmers in the heat.
The marquee occupies the upper right quadrant of
your vision. Lower, to the left, a man pushes a wheelbarrow, and in the wheelbarrow, yes, there is another
man, swathed in black, sopping up the force of the
hanging sun. Eyes. It is not possible to be alive and
suffer so, but the eyes are alive. Your first leper.

Inside, the clerk says, "Yes, miraculously, sa'ab, we
have a reservation for you." He salutes on every syllable. He sprints upstairs in the heat, saluting, because
the elevator operators are on strike. "Bad boys, sa'ab.
Very bad boys." He unlocks the door just before you
stumble in.

In the room, under the fan, panting, breathing
through your nose, trying to defend yourself against
the air. The clerk salutes, switches on the overhead
fan. You throw your arm across your face. The clerk
salutes, stares inquisitively, leaves.

He returns towing the young girl, still clutching her

infant. The clerk flings the girl at the side of the bed and shakes you by the shoulder. The clerk rips off her blouse. The infant is squalling. The clerk salutes.

"Nothing touch, sa'ab. Virgin Mary. Nothing touch."

You wave him away, dig for coins. The girl salutes. "Virgin Mary," she says. "Nothing touch."

Sleep comes often, a dreamless half-death. Nothing touch.

You wake in the morning and pace, frightened of the heat. The stench of unfamiliar fish is the prostitute, huddled in bed, nursing her child. Nothing touch. From the balcony you watch a fishing boat, its dagger sail nicking the sweet green rind of the Arabian sea. A gull kites backwards in the breeze, informing on schools of fish. Fleas are doing something desperate on your sleeve. Your mind shoots to a point near the hull where the sun is sparkling and the water gently slapping. Fish.

"Delhi. Bengal. Monsoon. Bombay." You toll the words aloud. "Bengal. Monsoon. Delhi. Bengal. Bombay. Monsoon."

Nothing touch.

Notre Dame was still getting smeared. Father Sullivan helped himself to more coleslaw. He dropped his fork. At breakfast he'd dropped it too. He'd made a nice save then before it actually hit the floor, though he hadn't been quick enough to escape an eschatological glance from Mrs. Garrity, the housekeeper. She was wise to him. Now the fork bounded out of reach under Father Cusack's chair.

Odd for Advent, but unmistakable: thunder rolled

overhead. Mrs. Garrity scowled at the drops streaming from the skylight. She set some pans out.

"A Protestant, in my opinion, is a man trying to tie his shoe while standing up," Father Cusack was saying. "He gets the job done but does it all wrong. A Protestant, however sincere, is off balance."

This concluded Father Cusack's commentary on the Ecumenical Movement. He fell into one of his casual trances and stared at the mayonnaise stain on Sullivan's copy of the *News*. Father Cusack, fresh out of Dunwoodie and the study of contradictions, had a flat, serious face; his forelock was combed across his brow like a shingle. His new mustache looked like eyelashes on a fish. Sullivan, inspired by the warm smells and the many hands, busy and freckled, which dominated the rectory dining room at lunch hour, drifted off into a trance of his own. Mrs. Garrity was serving chicken à la king again and not taking any guff about it. Thunder. Sullivan's beer, down to less than an inch from the bottom and having only a few stray comets of foam, quivered.

Monsignor MacMurray entered. Known in Stella Maris and beyond as Moose MacMurray, he still carried, at seventy-four, the frame of a breakaway fullback. He was a nice guy, loved to give and receive congratulations. When Father Cusack had inquired how one gets to rise in the ranks, Moose replied: "Just stick around."

"What quarter is it?" Monsignor MacMurray asked without taking his eyes off the television set.

"Third or fourth," Sullivan said, wondering if more coleslaw would materialize.

Monsignor MacMurray nodded like an auctioneer nodding at money. "Any first downs in this half?"

"Not a blessed one," Father Garafalo said, spooning

himself a modest amount of strawberry yogurt, which everybody knew he stashed in his room. Father Garafalo, not to be outdone by Sullivan's tropical cassock, was completely white: his hair was white, his shirt was white. So were his white shoes, white slacks and white cardigan. The effect was heightened by the color of his eyes, which were pink, like his yogurt. All in all, he was a tidy arrangement of griefs.

Monsignor MacMurray addressed himself to Sullivan: "I can't believe it, Jack."

"Yeah, Moose." Sullivan made an effort to search for subtleties in televised sport. "A tie ball game would have been hard to believe, but this is ridiculous."

"A priest is often a fan of the fanless," Father Cusack said, kicking Sullivan's fork without acknowledging it. "Lacrimae rerum, hey, Father?"

"Yup," Sullivan said.

"'The tears of things,'" Father Cusack translated fondly, needlessly. "Isn't that how Virgil put it, Father?"

"Yup." Sullivan wanted his fork.

"I'll confess I find the Evangelist's variation—lacrimae Christi—more . . . more . . . more . . ." Father Cusack was wobbling toward another trance. ". . . more stirring." There was in fact a *lacrima* of something in each of Father Cusack's blue eyes, which were customarily so clear as to suggest a transcendental state of eagerness. "White people, some of them," he was saying now, "white people starved to death right here in Brooklyn during the Depression. Were you aware of that, Father?"

"Yup."

By the time Cusack got to the point, he'd be saying it was okay for the sons and daughters of those starved white survivors to be dropping bombs on starving yellow Communists. Well, fine. All Cusack wanted was the luxury of hating like a rich man. He'd never quite make it, God bless him.

"All's I know about politics," Monsignor MacMurray said, scolding the rain and everything else, "is that this skylight was installed by anarchists."

Sullivan scratched his leg, which had just sent him an order to stretch. The cast had been off for a week. The doctor, when he took his electric saw to it, said, "This is going to stink," and it did, like cheese. The cast split open; shards of yellow skin helicoptered to the linoleum.

He scratched harder and wondered how much it would hurt to point his toes. My father's frozen breath, he thought, that's my politics. Passed out one night on the docks in Red Hook. Dead of pneumonia the next week. Pete Sullivan's boy Jack was two at the time.

He studies it, this essential sliver of his childhood: the chicken on the tip of his mother's serving fork. What is wrong? After months of eating chicken, there's only rice and coffee and there's something shrunken about this piece of chicken. He picks it off his fork, turns it over and over. His mother looks away, whistles a kiss to the parrot. This is a chicken back. Something for soup. No meat. Skin and bones, literally. No wonder he's cranky. He's going hungry. His mother glances at him shyly, the crossword pencil in her hair. "Eat it and be glad," she says.

How many comedians' mothers tell their kids you can't eat jokes? He doesn't want to hide, doesn't want to leave. Nobody can leave, unless it's for jail or the Marines or the cemetery. But it's *our* jail, *our* Marines, and, with the Church, *our* death. He is proud and sorry about being poor. He becomes a priest.

"Oh, by the way, yes," Father Cusack was saying. "Another thing occurs to me." He spread his fingers and walked them, like chubby spiders, across his temple. "I've been going over to the Catholic Worker and playing basketball with the Puerto Rican kids. There's this lay teacher from St. Francis giving emergency Spanish lessons in the evening. He's a widower; one of those guys, you know, that's ashamed of his drinking. He spends a lot of time in class analyzing the difference between *ser* and *estar*. But as far as the language goes, I'll tell you, as soon as those Spicks start playing ball, all they say is *aquí, aquí*. And I'll tell you another thing: they tend to be short."

"Hey Cusack," Monsignor MacMurray said. "Hire a hall, why dontcha?"

Five

The streetlights sparkled; the eastern horizon was red. Heaven was still a deep marine blue.

Priests and doctors saw a lot of dawns. Father Sullivan was a great lover of dawns, particularly in the Northeast, where they were a time of privacy and prayer. In this part of the world he treasured the day's calm ignition, so unlike the tropics, where the sun popped up like a bubble and burst, full of chatter.

Freddy Powers sat behind the wheel of his rebuilt Land Rover and waved his only arm. The driver of the Leyland tanker, his collarbone shattered and his career ruined, had walked away with the right one.

Sullivan felt a shyness; they clasped left hands. The vacant right sleeve of Freddy's bush jacket was safety-pinned at his shoulder. On the sidewalk, a pigeon came in for a landing and skidded on a patch of ice. They were both looking that way and they both chuckled. Freddy punched the dashboard. The radio went on, something by Smokey Robinson and the Miracles, high and loud.

"That's the only thing they couldn't fix." He patted his knee. "Well, not the only thing."

His feet dangled straight down. Affectionately he pushed them away from the accelerator and brake. He raised his hand and gunned the handicap control lever on the steering column.

Cripples have shiny shoes, Sullivan noticed. He recognized the case for Freddy's old birdwatching scope, stitched together from a couple of firearm holsters. In the backseat, efficiently restrained by plastic tiedowns, were his guitar case and his wheelchair. But a guitar took two hands.

The invitation had come on one of Freddy's old Christmas cards, featuring a picture of himself in a cowboy outfit on a palomino pony, bucking, waving a ten-gallon hat in one hand, the other tucking the reins to his chest. Four Leicas with lenses of different lengths were slung around his neck. On either side of the picture was the printed text: a list of the models, serial numbers and country of origin of all his camera equipment, along with their approximate value in American dollars. This was Freddy's customs manifest, printed in bulk because of the many times he had to present it at the many borders he used to cross, a rich kid starved for necessities. On the back he'd written that he and Natalie had returned to the States in time for Christmas and they'd love to see him. Natalie was teaching Comp Lit at Bard ("The Woman and the Serpent from the Pre-Socratics to Camus") and she was upstate looking for a farm to buy. Freddy could pick him up while running an errand in Brooklyn.

The sky lightened, a bright slate. The breeze stiffened. The Verrazano Bridge, caissons pillowed in mist, sailed by. They passed Sheepshead Bay and Coney Island without a word, the parachute jump towering above the boardwalk, solitary and familiar, like the occasional appearance of a king. Still they were silent, though Sullivan knew he was in a carload of ventriloquists, their dummy the dawn. The steering wheel began to shake in Freddy's hand; the Land Rover shimmied.

It was just seven when they pulled up at the garage. The sign said: MILITARY ANTIQUES WANTED.

"Hey Mitch!" Freddy shouted. "How're you doing?"

A German shepherd yelped. She had yellow targety eyes and her coat was greasy from sleeping under the hoist.

"Hey Mitch! Hey Mitch! You got the plow for this thing yet?"

Mitch had seven ballpoint pens in the top pocket of his overalls and he was dragging a dolly heaped with transmission gears. "Not yet," he said. He was a man of many smiles.

The shepherd bolted from his side and charged the Land Rover, barking and leaping as high as the window, paws rattling on Freddy's door. Freddy punched the dashboard, silencing the radio, and rolled his window halfway down.

"How about the power takeoff?" Freddy shouted.

Mitch shook his head no. He fingered his bottle-thick glasses as if tuning a special instrument of speech. The shepherd barked and barked and barked.

"Hey Mitch! You got that Magnum yet?"

"Down, Simone," Mitch said. "Good girl."

Simone fell back, whining, and snapped at her tail.

"Come on around back," Mitch said. "I got to park my car."

Freddy lowered himself into the wheelchair. "That's

okay," he said to Sullivan, brushing him away from the handles. "I got it now." He propelled himself through a puddle, then stopped to wipe his hand on his pants. "Look at me. JesusMaryanJoseph, am I dumb."

Simone peed on a four-cylinder crankshaft and nosed them around the corner, her tongue steaming in the cold.

They beheld a pyramid of junked cars, mostly VW's, snouts in the air like dying beasts.

"Oh great," Freddy said. "He's got it. This is terrific."

The Magnum was a rather ordinary piece of metal-work—Sullivan had expected something theatrical, glossy—it was a dull gray club for killing, that was all. Mitch cradled it across his palms. "Now I'm gonna park my car," he said.

"What car?" Freddy said.

"That one." Mitch waved the Magnum in the direction of the junk pile. He turned slowly, widened his stance and gripped the gun with both hands, raising it from stomach level. When it reached a point on a line with his nose, he squeezed the trigger.

The muzzle flash made Sullivan blink. He blinked again at the pop and the high-pitched ping: the full force of the shot was beyond audible range. Sullivan felt a gonging in his sinuses, then, between his shoulder blades, something like a tap. There was a brief tearing noise from the white Beetle on top of the pile, followed by a sprinkling of glass.

"Let me try it," Freddy said. "Let me try it."

Mitch pressed Freddy's hand into position.

"Relax. The whole thing is to relax."

Freddy fired, the cars clanged. The recoil spun his wheelchair to the right and the gun went off again, apparently by mistake. The second round plowed up the mud at the base of the outhouse. Simone circled.

"It'll do that," Mitch said. "You got to lock your wheels and relax on the backfire."

Mitch smiled at Sullivan. "You wanna try it? It'll be a nice thing to have when those Commie Chinks come over the hill."

Sullivan said nothing. It took an effort of the will, renewed from instant to instant, to remind him that he was not a bystander at a repeat performance of the car crash.

Mitch pulled off three professionally spaced rounds. The white Beetle tipped, slumped a few inches. Simone was doing something shrewd with her nose.

"That's the way we park a car in East Canarsie." He broke the gun down, snap-clack, and packed it away in a case resembling a doctor's satchel. "I can't let you have this one. It's a demonstrator. I got some on order."

"When are you getting them?" Freddy said.

"Call me."

"Okay. What about the plow?"

"Next week maybe."

"I'll call you next week. Thanks a lot, Mitch."

The Land Rover bucked. Freddy restarted the engine. It stalled again and Sullivan's knee slammed into the low-range lever: more gnashing. Freddy punched the dashboard. "Mustang Sally!" he screamed. "Come on now, baby." He jabbed it again. His vacant sleeve came unpinned. "Shit. It's really busted now."

Sullivan punched it. A burst of static, then nothing.

"Try a little holy water, Father." Freddy repinned his sleeve, smiling. "So how you been, Jack?"

Sullivan let go a sigh of fear-impacted memory. He

tapped his leg and thought of the days they'd spent stalking peacocks in the Rajasthan dunes. Certain homosexual relationships must be truly romantic: two men reliving their boyhoods, taking each other to fine restaurants, courting each other with talk about the objects they loved. Seeing your past, your youth in another man—that was something you couldn't do with women, those tangled trees. "I feel great," Sullivan said.

"That's good. You look great. A little weird. But great."

"*Me* weird?"

They laughed, sharing a ridiculous memory of themselves in *khadi pajamini* and sandals. The truth, Sullivan knew, was that Freddy, being from Boston rather than Brooklyn, did not look up to priests. Boston Catholics looked *down* at priests, tolerated them fondly, like shooting dogs valued for the special virtues of their breed. Freddy was a rich kid with standards instead of politics; Sullivan was a poor kid with a license to preach. It would always be painful for each of them to admit what he really wanted. In India, before the accident, Sullivan had watched Natalie thrive while Freddy went politely crazy. He'd lost weight and become pleadingly loyal. He took to sleeping in the Land Rover, which he parked by the holding tank. He and Natalie were kind to one another; he learned to seek her shade. But Sullivan had always been certain Natalie kept a secret plan of escape which included him. And about this his conscience no longer felt like a tooth especially sensitive to the cold. Interesting women were truly expensive: you had to earn them. Expensive and salty.

A cloud of seagulls pounced on the garbage dump

straight ahead. Freddy punched the radio. Nothing. His head drooped forward with the weight of what he was about to say:

"I guess we both made bad marriages, Jack."

"Yup."

"Listen, Jack. I'm totally out of it, okay?"

"Sure. Okay."

Together they pounded on the dashboard until the news coughed up something about 400,000 American boys being in Vietnam before the end of the year, as if God were still wasting our time.

Sister Marian pressed her knees into the pew with a force that seemed to come from outside her.

"Mother most chaste," she said, "mother inviolable, mother undefiled, mother most amiable, mother of good counsel, mother of our creator, mother of our savior, virgin most prudent, virgin most venerable, virgin most renowned, virgin most powerful, virgin most merciful, virgin most faithful, mirror of justice, seat of wisdom, cause of our joy, spiritual vessel, vessel of honor, singular vessel of devotion, mystical rose, tower of David, tower of ivory, house of gold, ark of the covenant, gate of heaven, morning star, health of the sick, refuge of sinners, comforter of the afflicted, help of Christians, queen of angels, queen of patriarchs, queen of prophets, queen of apostles, queen of martyrs, queen of confessors, queen of virgins, queen of all saints, pray for me."

She examined her new watch, a birthday present from Aunt Bea, the Protestant from Portland. In another ten minutes she was due for her appointment *chez* Sister Superior. The watch, for its part, looked cheerful: its tiny gold-and-white face, nested in blue enamel, the winding stem jutting out, stalklike, always loose, reminded Marian of something Dutch. She used to wonder why no one else in the convent, where schedules were so important, wore a watch. It was not because the Sisters told time by the bells; the bells were a mess. The minute Sister Marian saw her watch, so excruciatingly little-girlish, she understood. Aunts may want nieces to know what time it is, even in the willed eternity of their little-girlhoods, but the only thing is, the nieces don't want to know, they just don't want to know. Lately she'd been wearing it to bed.

"Impone, Domine, capiti meo galeam salutis," Father Sullivan said. "Place, O Lord, the helmet of salvation on my head, ad expugnandos diabolicos incursus. So I can overcome the assaults of the devil."

The sacristy, where the altar boys' rehearsals were being held, was a large room of dark woods: teak chests in which the vestments were folded, and mahogany walls with a cool, oiled look, and highlights steady as the eyes of hunting trophies, shining evenly in the low illumination, inviting touch. The call for new altar boys had been posted on all the bulletin boards the morning of Ember Wednesday, a day set aside for penance in the form of prayer and fasting, signified by the deep violet vestments adorning the priests that day at Mass. This was not nearly as dramatic, though, as Ash Wednesday, when everyone strutted around showing off the smudges on their foreheads. Ashes to ashes. Peanuts got a kick out of this decorative attitude toward death, though on Jewel Cherry Jackson's chocolate forehead the ashes were clearly just dirt.

"For purity and strength," Father Sullivan said. He was washing his fingers in a small wooden bowl. He took off his jacket, unfastened his collar and unbuttoned his shirt. He was not physically impressive, but in the dimness, each muscle flicked.

"The alb is a figure of perfect integrity." He read from a corpulent book dripping with satin markers. He slipped a white gown over his head; it hissed. He held up a braided rope and tied it around his waist. "Gird me, O Lord, with the cincture of purity and extinguish in my loins the desire of lust, so that the virtues of continence and chastity may ever abide with me." He draped a napkin over his left wrist.

"This maniple formerly served the purpose of a handkerchief, and reminds us that it is our lot on earth to sow tears."

Bad John Maguire, camouflaging a sneer with his first baseman's mitt, shouldered through the door and dukewayned his way toward Peanuts. Bad John was fourteen, the oldest fifth-grader. Next year they'd have to promote him whether he learned to read or not. For him it was going to be jail or the Marines. "Baseball's almost here," he said, flipping Peanuts a baseball, an immaculate regulation model from the carton he'd boosted last night. Peanuts caught it and tossed it back; Bad John scooped it in his mitt.

The others—Ferrugia, Dewey, Shea, Noonan, Nolan and the Donnellys, all three of them, stinking and sockless—were looking at Father Sullivan, and Father Sullivan was looking at his chasuble, a dazzling sleeveless robe, laying it out with an assurance that was partly magical, partly military. Crazy Doyle, wearing wood-wheeled roller skates which so far had escaped detection, choked back a giggle. Crazy Doyle, skating toward expulsion.

"Hey Father," Richie Frevola said, "when do we get *our* outfits?" Richie was a fat kid and everybody loved to pinch his ass because his mother and father, who'd made a bundle in their ornamental-railing business, dressed him in silk shorts, so your fingers would slide around when you goosed him.

"Your outfits, yeah," Father Sullivan said. "You'll get your cassock and surplice as soon as you learn your Latin. You're the last class that'll have to know it, but you're going to get it right, as long as I have anything to do with it. And when you get your cassocks, try not to trip over them. You supply your own black shoes. Black socks, too. No loafers, no sneakers out there in the altar. DeFazio, get the gum out of your mouth."

Tommy DeFazio plucked an enormous pink wad, fleshy and alive-looking, from between his molars.

"And stick it on your forehead."

"Oh Jesus, Father . . ."

"Oh Jesus is right," Father Sullivan said. Everybody breathed easy. He was a man, a foreign missionary, a stranger; he was tolerant of savage ways, easy on bad language and venial sins of impetuosity.

The chasuble whispered to the other vestments when Father Sullivan slipped it over his head. It was the color of a red rose in shade. On the outside, front and back—so that the priest when he turned looked like a sign with identical sides—the Sisters had outlined a rosy cross with red and silver stitches, each stitch the tongue of a small flower. Father Sullivan was a towering map of black lands and crimson wars, their tiny silver victories, their pink defeats.

"Now, if everybody's got a copy of the words for himself," he said, "we might as well go through it on the altar."

Peanuts was reminded, as they crowded through the door, that Father Sullivan, for all his vestments, was nothing more than a man with a limp, and Peanuts wondered if his stutter was the same.

The taps on Bad John's shoes echoed brilliantly on the way to the altar. Crazy Doyle, last in line, tiptoed on his roller skates, uncannily quiet. Peanuts realized he'd have to give some thought to the rhythm of his walk too because the vault of the church caught every step, every knee shifting in every pew, every prayer, mumble, cough and sneeze, and held them all like baffled smoke.

He looked up, past the Bernini bronzes, following echoes toward the tall painting that stood behind the altar like the sky over a faded garden. It was the Immaculate Conception, three times life size at least. The Virgin, draped in a gown that seemed to lift rather than restrain her, was stepping on a small crescent moon, just lightly touching it with her sandals. In a robin's-egg-blue sky with yolky clouds there were little angels, hands folded over their hearts, eyes rolling upward, and around the Virgin's head was a halo of softly burning stars. Her scarf was fluttering in the heavenly breeze, exciting another flock of *putti,* their skins all gold. It was a painting of air and light.

The painting was flanked by long marble panels, slimmer than the mural but just as tall. The marble was veined like cross sections of clouds in which the bones of giant warriors were embedded. In the choir loft at the far end of the church, the organist was testing his bellows: low sustained notes growled through the vault as his fingers searched from key to key.

"Now there's a note that'll loosen your fillings, gentlemen." Father Sullivan crossed in front of the tabernacle and genuflected, despite his limp, in that loose, jointless way that came from years of it. "All right, take your cards."

He held up a plastic-laminated sheet of paper identical to the ones Peanuts and the others found on the eight-sided table made entirely of ruby-colored glass. Candlelight glinted off the gold borders of Peanuts' card as he angled it in an attempt to make sense of the Latin, which was lettered in red. The English translation, in black on the other side, was dim and hard to make out, distracted as he was by a fierce flipping of cards from Latin to English, English to Latin.

"There's no rush, now," Father Sullivan said. "The whole thing is to relax." He made the sign of the cross on his chest, the tips of his fingers scuffing against the silken cross.

"In nomine patris et filii et spiritus sancti, amen ..."

Slowly he extended his arms and looked straight ahead, then slowly, slowly down, he brought his hands together to a cushioned stop.

"Introibo ad altare Dei ..."

He took a half-step back, hands still joined.

"Response, men," he said, speaking over his shoulder. It took a second for Peanuts to translate the sound of his words—so exalted, anonymous and sudden—into ordinary Brooklyn sense.

"Response. All together now. Read the first response. Look at your cards. The first line on the red side is where you'll find it. It goes this way: I say, 'Introibo ad

altare Dei' and you say—pay attention to your cards—
'Ad Deum qui laetificat juventutem meam.' " Father
Sullivan poised his finger like a baton. "Let's go."

His hand dropped. There was a general mumble-
hum. Peanuts licked the cold salt sweat from his upper
lip. He swallowed. Bad John pulled out a water pistol
and drilled Crazy Doyle between the eyes. Crazy Doyle
quivered, but managed, by stiffening his whole body
and grabbing DeFazio's belt, not to rattle his roller
skates. DeFazio was chewing like a maniac again, the
first wad riding rhythmically up and down between his
eyebrows.

"Okay, lovely," Father Sullivan said, oblivious.
"Now let's take it one at a time. Kennedy, go ahead."

Peanuts looked down at his card. He saw red lines.
He turned it over. He saw black lines. Wax plopped
from the candles.

"Let's hear it now," Father Sullivan said. "After me,
Kennedy. And the rest of you pay attention. I say the
Latin, Kennedy responds, then we all do it together.
Got it? Introibo ad altare Dei. The gum, DeFazio, the
gum! Someplace else, please—the gum!"

DeFazio made room on his forehead for a second wad.
He now had the pink supernumerary eyes of an altar
boy from outer space.

"Okay," Father Sullivan said. "Introibo ad altare
Dei . . . I go to the altar of God . . . ad Deum qui laetificat
juventutem meam . . . to God, who brings joy to my
youth."

Peanuts thought the low clicking noise had something to do with Bad John's water pistol, but when he
looked, it wasn't Bad John he saw. It was Sister
Marian, kneeling in the Sisters' chapel to the side of
the main altar. The clicking . . . the clicking was rosary

beads. What was odd, though, for someone saying the rosary, was the smile on Sister Marian's face. Father Sullivan did not notice her.

"Response, Kennedy. Are we going to hear from you today?"

Peanuts dropped his plastic card and raised his arms, winglike, as Father Sullivan had done.

"Uruguay," he said.

Father Sullivan's face went perfectly still. For a moment Peanuts thought he saw in it the merciful amnesiac pity stutterers so often see. Father Sullivan followed Peanuts' eyes to Sister Marian. He recovered instantly and turned back to the boys.

"Lovely," he said. "Lovely, lovely. But next time, Kennedy, let's have it without the arms, okay? Next man. Doyle, where are you?"

Bad John, looking at his feet and concealing the water pistol under his armpit, drenched Crazy Doyle's shirtfront, and it was all over. Crazy Doyle staggered, tottered, windmilled and crashed across the marble steps, totally out of control, skates clattering, zinging on key with the organist, suddenly panicked also, arpeggios in pursuit. Crazy Doyle.

"Who committed her?" Sister Superior said.

She was on the phone. Her knuckles were enormous. She was seventy-one years of age. Today her door was propped open by *A Treasury of French Impressionism.*

Sister Marian perched on the damasked armchair in her office. Through the curtains, the clouds were unhealthy sections of vapor. The light was gold, petals of the sunset caroming off the windows of the sporting goods store across the street. Very soon, on the upholstery, there would be only the shine of streetlights, but it was understood that no one would turn on a lamp.

Pinned over her left breast, Sister Superior wore a green-and-red Christmas wreath braided of bright yarn, swelling and shrinking like a small externalized organ of circulation. She put down the receiver and fingered a vacant bud vase.

"Excuse me," she said. "When you got a phone, you gotta phone."

Sister Marian and Sister Superior laughed simultaneously. Sister Superior's laugh changed pitch suddenly, though. She looked at Sister Marian as at someone who might have behaved badly in a dream.

Jasper, the white female Manx who seemed more than wise, stepped out of Sister Superior's lap in search of the retreating sun. Instead of a tail, Jasper had a stump which she circulated when excited, like an absent thumb. Marian observed her settling on Sister Superior's desk next to a photograph of Archbishop Boyle, which was autographed in a spidery regal hand. Sister Superior nudged the picture frame back an inch or two, downshifting the tone of her laugh still further.

"Jasper has the poor taste to prefer men," Sister Superior said. "Given the chance. When weighed against the business of getting on with one's life, though, men have little to recommend them. The business of one's life, Sister. What *is* the business of life?" She swiveled her chair and lowered the volume of "La Vie en Rose" on her Victrola. "We don't need men, Sister. We need conductors. Do you mind if I smoke?"

"Oh n-n-n-no. Not at all." Sister Marian braced the brass elephant lighter in both hands.

Sister Superior inhaled deliciously. The tarry smell of her Gauloise seeped everywhere. "Sidewalks of a certain age," she had commented during one of their get-acquainted strolls, "Sidewalks d'un certain âge. See the wrinkles?" Sister Superior had studied art for a semester in Paris. She swiveled toward the window.

"Ah, Paris," she said. She crossed something off a legal pad. "Mint, Sister?" She urged a fluted glass bowl full of candies across her desk.

Marian's fingernail pierced the foil and dug into the chocolate. She licked her finger.

"Are you happy with the food here?" Sister Superior asked.

"Yes, I like it, Sister." The Gauloise smoke pawed her.

"Do you, Sister? The water is not very satisfying. Of course, there's really nothing to be done for the sadness and nastiness of physical decline, I suppose. Sauve qui peut." Sister Superior smiled, apparently in the direction of Jasper, who was keeping herself concealed from Sister Marian.

With a sudden rustle of her habit, Sister Superior rose and rolled up her sleeve. Marian, in a reflex of self-defense, also got to her feet.

"I want to show you something," Sister Superior said. "Come closer, Sister."

Sister Superior bunched the sleeve above her left elbow and leaned under the desk lamp. "Go ahead, Sister, turn it on."

The bulb blinked, went off. Marian got a firmer grip on the switch and turned it slowly.

Sister Superior's forearm was bluish and meaty. The tattoo on the underside was a crown of thorns on top of a heart, very large, almost life size. Sister Superior made a fist, opened her hand, made a fist again. The tattooed heart beat in time with her hand.

"It's lovely, Sister," Marian said. She meant it. The tattooed heart, something about its simplicity and optimism, had a calming effect.

"Thank you, Sister. I was wondering how to improve it. It needs something . . . maybe an arrow. Or a chain. What do you think?" Her eyelids fluttered like the pages of a book.

"A chain, Sister?"

"Well yes, Sister. I've always felt like a slave." Sister Superior rolled down her sleeve and switched off the light, massaging her arm. "Jasper? J'espère?"

The cat, now blue-gray in the darkness, stared at Sister Superior over her shoulder, shrugging twice. Sister Superior went to the bookcase and picked her up, furred liquid pouring backward.

"How is Dr. Jimmy?" she asked.

"I'm not sure, Sister."

"Of course. Dr. Jimmy is fine, Sister. Dr. Jimmy is just fine." Sister Superior schmoozed to Jasper. "It's all right. I just spoke with him. He recommended this marvelous young woman who's learning tattoos. We discussed what kind of tattoo I should have next. She suggested an angel or a unicorn. Don't care for unicorns myself."

"How about a sea horse, Sister?"

Sister Superior removed her finger from Jasper's ear. "What is a sea horse but a wet unicorn, Sister?" She began to stroll. "How about a mermaid with a heartbreaking smile? That's more like it, don't you think? But what do I know? Do you know who my favorite artist is?"

"Yes, Sister. I mean, who?"

"Sonja Henie."

"Wow, Sister. She's some skater. I've seen her on The Late Show, I think."

"Yes, I know. *Sun Valley Serenade,* right?" Sister Superior unloaded Jasper on the carpet and placed another Gauloise between her lips.

"Guy Mitchell," Marian said. "He's *my* favorite. 'Heartaches by the Number'—I love the way he whistles that."

"All right, Sister." This time Sister Superior lit the cigarette herself, snapping the elephant lighter eight times without accelerating the tempo of her squeezes, setting it finally on a doily next to the Archbishop's portrait, where it toppled noiselessly. She pushed back the drapes: a spoiled orange light bloomed in the room.

"I've been a Sister of the Blessed Heart for forty-three years, Sister. But I keep in touch. Many of my girlfriends still visit. Very often they bring their grandchildren." She peered at Marian as if verifying the arrival of each word in her heart. Her eyes were brimming, perhaps because of the smoke. She used both hands to remove the cigarette from her mouth; the paper stuck to her lips.

"People who live without physical love," she continued, "people like you and me, Sister, after a while, we tend to need . . . after a certain period of deprivation . . ." Sister Superior exhaled the next word on top of her cigarette smoke. ". . . after a certain period of deprivation, after despair, you'll find it becomes necessary, Sister, to construct a version of your life which says, 'This is okay, I'm satisfied.' As brides of Christ, we pledge to God our affections, even those we might not be aware of. I, as I have said, have always felt like a slave. So did Teresa of Avila. You may smile at the comparison, Sister. 'Esclavita' is what St. Teresa called herself. It's usually translated as 'handmaiden,' as if she were talking about a rank in a royal household, but 'slave' is what St. Teresa said. Sister Marian, what I have to say to you is this: you may have the emotions of a daughter, but I wonder if you are truly a slave."

Sister Superior lit a fresh Gauloise from the old one and shut the drapes. It was a farewell gesture from someone who was used to having her judgments attended to. Marian lowered her head. What time is it? she wondered addictively. She plucked at her watch stem. Until this moment she had always imagined herself too . . . too ordinary to be free. But it wasn't so, it wasn't so. He loved her—that was so. Any child could see it. Her ankles ached from wanting to dance.

Peanuts Kennedy became the perfect altar boy.

All he could say was "Uruguay," and he understood very little of the Latin, but who did, anyway? He served Mass only with Father Sullivan, who didn't seem to care what he said.

Father Sullivan took all the new altar boys on a field trip to St. Patrick's Cathedral by way of the Frick Museum, where he stood for a full ten minutes in front of Rembrandt's *Polish Rider*. Crazy Doyle got himself kicked out for rollerskating around the fountain.

The *Polish Rider,* the young soldier on horseback— that was the kind of missionary Peanuts wanted to be. He had a quiver, he had a sword, a scabbard, gold boots, and he had gold stirrups. And the gold light, groping— the kindness of it. But the horse, the horse headed grimly into the storm, nostrils flared, uncertain whose side he would choose when the thunderclap came—the rider's or the sky's. And on the shore of the muddy lake, was that a campfire? Or a cannon? The painting moved.

Afterward, Father Sullivan bought everybody ice cream at the Blarney Stone; he chased down his vanilla fudge with four quick beers, never inquiring whatever happened to his switchblade.

Moose MacMurray asked Mrs. Garrity to place another call to Sister Superior. He kept one eye on the Knicks game.

"Look, Marilyn, all I'm saying is I think maybe it's time you had another little chat with her, that's all. I mean, they're out there playing catch in the schoolyard."

"Now?"

The smack of ball-in-mitt carried from the yard below. Mrs. Garrity topped off the Monsignor's glass with the last few drops she could find in any can of Rheingold.

"Yes, now," the Monsignor said.

"Oh yeah? How's her stuff?"

"Now just cut out the Flying Nun crap, okay, please Marilyn? I mean in the *schoolyard,* for crying out loud."

Mrs. Garrity leaned out the window for a good look. She swayed back inside, invoking the Holy Family.

"Oh, wet suffering Jesus," she said. "Just look at the

two of them, will you? Now all of a sudden it's the nuns that're in a big hurry for it, too!"

"Mrs. Garrity!" Moose said. "Please!"

Incessant coughing said the church was full.

Then the organ moaned, the choir boomed. Even in Latin, the singing sounded military. The closest Peanuts came to recognizing any of the words was something that sounded like "Domino Poughkeepsie." He imagined, shifting from one foot to another, that his gleaming gold candlestick was a baseball bat sacred to wise-guy angels who used it solely for swatting ground rule doubles. He stared into the guttering flame. The choir sang. Two down, angel on second. He swung. The choir cheered. "Domino Poughkeepsie."

For half an hour, for most of the Midnight Mass, he held the candlestick, tall as himself, and when the great bell bonged its fullest peal, he floated away on the perfume of lilies and incense and old parishioners' ardent sweat. Actually, the bell did not bong, peal or toll. It was a city church; it clanged.

Uruguay. Uruguay. Uruguay.

Sister Marian loved the smell of makeup. On top of her coronet she placed the chartreuse shag wig, styled for her from a bath mat by Sister Sheila, the fashion plate. While smearing on more clownwhite, she told the class about clowns, how no two were alike, that their makeup was a sort of trademark. Other thoughts she kept to herself (children don't want to know everything): does the habit of laughter prepare us for martyrdom?

She began to hate her audience. She was an old Bozo, ancient, in pain, half-blind and deaf in one ear, so that she had to turn one way to hear and another to see. She saved herself by jumping up, transformed at last. The class applauded.

"So don't forget, boys and girls, that Jesus was a clown, too. Lose your life to find it, he said." Marian crushed the wig in her lap. "A clown, besides having a sense of humor, must have the ability to mask personal pain. A good clown can calm people down in the event of a circus fire, and there have been recorded instances of this actually taking place. How many of you would like to be a clown for today?"

Everybody's hand went up, except Dirty Dot's, whose hands were elsewhere.

"Dorothy?"

The bell caught Marian by surprise, but not Peanuts. She stopped him before he got through the door. He pulled away; she still had greasepaint on her hands.

"Maybe we'll hear from you next time, Mr. Kennedy."

Peanuts nodded.

"Look, Dennis, I just got another letter from Sister Augusta." Marian flapped an envelope striped with gaudy stamps. She pointed to a wall map captioned FOREIGN MISSIONS, *Less Polar Regions*. The map, its lacquer cracked like old clay, was sprinkled with pins.

"You remember, Dennis, how in her last letter Sister Augusta wrote about the noises llamas make. How the llamas *talk* is how she put it, if I'm not mistaken."

"Hmmm . . ." Peanuts said.

"Yes, Dennis. Talk. The llamas sound just like a little what?" Marian spoke with her hands.

"Mmmm . . ."

"A little foghorn, that's right. Sister Augusta's got
such a way with words. Also, Dennis, she said what else
about the llamas? They . . . what? When they see people
wearing glasses, the llamas . . ."

"Ssss . . ."

"Spit! That's right. They spit, the llamas do, whenever they see someone wearing glasses. Imagine that!
Well, very good, Dennis. You're making progress, real
progress. Stuttering is one of Almighty God's many
mysteries, isn't it, Dennis? Nobody knows what causes
it really. It's almost like a miracle. You remember the
definition of a miracle from your catechism, I'm sure."

She nodded encouragement while Peanuts shaped
the words after her.

"That's right . . . a manifestation of the infinite
mercy and wisdom of Almighty God. A mysterious
manifestation of the infinite mercy and wisdom of Almighty God. That's very good, very good." She laid her
hand on the map. "And Sister Augusta is where, Dennis?"

"P-pride," he said.

Sister Marian fingered the moment like a glass ball
he'd tossed her.

"Yes, pride. That was very good." She began to walk
in a circle, her habit twirling. "Yes, Father Sullivan
gets very tired sometimes. Father is used to strange
pagan ways. Sometimes Father forgets he's talking to
little children." She slipped her hands under her bib.
Her eyes softened. "All of us, Dennis, have hopes and
dreams we pray to Almighty God to answer. I myself

have prayed, often prayed, to serve alongside Sister Augusta, raising silkworms in the hills of you-know-where and saving souls."

Peanuts knew all about Sister Augusta: what flowers flourished in the coolness of her Uruguayan garden, where the mangoes ripened first, what she thought about rock 'n' roll (she was a Jerry Lee Lewis fan). He knew also that when Sister Marian spoke of Sister Augusta she was talking about herself. Sister Marian's heart was a conspicuous secret, the kind kids love to keep.

She stopped pacing as if she'd bumped into a wall. "The cocoons, don't you imagine, Dennis, must be very beautiful. The spinning of their silk . . . silkworms eat mulberry leaves." She moved again. "But not all the foreign missions are so far away, are they now, Dennis? We can each of us be foreign missionaries right here in Brooklyn, can't we? Brooklyn is unique. Brooklyn is the only diocese in the world completely within city limits, did you know that? But each of you children in class is a foreign mission to me." She smiled and drifted back to the map. "I think of you more than you know, Dennis." She searched the map, uncertain. "As I'm sure you think of me, I mean, more than I know." Her eyes found the spot. "And now tell me where Sister Augusta and the silkworms are, Dennis."

"P-p-pride," he said.

"No, Dennis. You remember. You can say it. Take your time." Marian tapped the pinks and greens of South America. "Now tell me where Sister Augusta and the silkworms are."

"Pride."

"Oh no, Dennis. N-n-n-no, no, no."

Six

"I'm freezing," Natalie Powers said from the front seat of the Land Rover. They'd picked her up outside the produce market on Ninth Avenue, after Freddy collected Father Sullivan and Sister Marian.

She greeted everybody with armloads of food. When she stepped out from behind her packages, Sullivan was astonished to see she'd put on a few pounds and seemed unaccountably shorter.

She'd suffered only bruises in the accident, a scar that left the right side of her jaw looking hinged, an artfully chipped front tooth, and a scalp cut that cost her a braid. She still wore sweaters, still moved swiftly, still was soft, still was alive under her clothes. And she had a tan, something she never came close to in India, though her nose was red from blowing it.

"Try it." She thrust a pale spiky vegetable in Sullivan's face. "It's raw."

She said ouch when he kissed her.

———

"Aren't you cold?" Marian said, snuggling closer.

Sullivan put his arm around her. The back of the Land Rover was laid out like a bus, seats along the sides. They sat on the floor, on Marian's sleeping bag, their backs vibrating against the front seat. Sullivan felt undignified and awkwardly displayed, like an old glider at the Smithsonian.

Freddy began singing "Michael, Row Your Boat Ashore." Sullivan and Natalie joined in, just as they'd done in the Jaipur mission, and when the song was over—only Marian's scandalously professional harmony carried into an extra chorus—Freddy said he'd never sing that cornball song again, just as he always did in Jaipur. By the time they left the Taconic Parkway, the fields were white and the wind was lashing tufts of snow from the hood. Natalie, a little hoarse, explained to Marian the difficulties of encouraging essentially tribal people to settle down in cooperative agriculture.

Sullivan studied the blue makeup around Natalie's eyes, disapproved of the way it compromised the exceptional frankness of her face and decided it was pathetic, the way she had chosen to be bogus.

Marian sat up straight and laced her fingers in her lap. "When I was sixteen, I won a scholarship to Radcliffe."

"Really?" Natalie said.

"I stuck it out for a whole year. I was miserable. Everybody's name was Mitzi or Bette with an e. I corresponded with Heidegger. He wrote me a note that I was the only one in the whole world who understood him and would I call on him in Germany. I had hair on my legs when nobody had hair on their legs. I sent him a snapshot. I took Russian. Odin malchik brosil nyatch ni provilno e raspil oknof parikmarherskoy. 'The boy threw the football incorrectly and broke the barbershop window.' "

"Really?" Freddy said.

"Yes. My vocation came all of a sudden, during Easter recess."

"The Tribals see cooperative systems as antagonistic, I think, to their religious beliefs," Natalie said. She went on with a brief analysis of chore-sharing among the Sikhs.

"Oh, but wouldn't it be nice if we could all live like that?" Marian said.

"Yeah," Sullivan interrupted, appalled at the sarcasm rippling involuntarily in his throat. "That would be nice."

He hadn't realized he'd be so jealous of the way Marian was hearing about India. He'd approached her in the middle of the schoolyard, just as she was dragging the Kennedy kid, the one who stuttered, away from a brawl about yoyos. He presented her with a copy of his book—*Water Table, Recent Poems*—inscribed "To Sister Silkworm: a terrible beauty is born," and asked her to go out with him. "God help you if you don't mean it," she'd said, and he'd laughed. The scandal was no big deal. The expectation that she might be sharing his secrets, though—that unsettled him.

Now Freddy was on about the unfairness of hereditary syphilis, which was endemic among the Tribals.

"Only an Irish Catholic of Jack Kennedy's class would call life merely unfair," Natalie said.

For a distance of three telephone poles—nearly four hundred feet—Sullivan watched a small bird flying parallel to the car with a field mouse in its beak. The mouse swayed. A truck hissed by and the bird veered

off. Animals do the real work, he thought, and don't
bitch about it.

Freddy, whistling gallantly, clanked up the pathway
with Natalie and Marian on either side, their arms
half-extended in the manner of backup vocalists. His
legs were strong enough for him to be using a walking
frame now.

Sullivan himself stepped carefully, sinking through
the soft fresh snow, crunching next through a thick
plate of ice and down finally to a packed base, each
layer giving way in a slightly different direction. The
sensation was of treading on enormous soft coins.

"Please don't toss cigarettes on the snow, Jack,"
Freddy said. "When it melts, you see them on the
lawn."

The Powers' farmhouse, fringed with a stand of blue
Norwegian firs, its second story freshly painted orange,
presented itself like a photographic irony. There was
no part of the world except India where such colors
would not be excruciating. Ducks from the pond con-
voyed overhead, close enough for the squeaking of their
wings to be a surprise. Somewhere, off in the Hudson,
ice was snapping and booming, and farther north, an
Erie whistle sounded, a moo from the phantom American herd.

Inside the house, Sullivan felt less plausible than the
furniture, which amounted to three derelict chairs and
an Edwardian sofa disemboweled by vermin. A hand-
tinted view of the Polo Grounds hung lopsidedly over
the fireplace.

"We better get some firewood." Marian rubbed the
sleeves of her parka, producing a high nylon whistle.

"What are you doing?" Sullivan said.

"Women in movies always go like this when it's cold." She smiled at herself, kept rubbing.

Sullivan caught a glimpse of Freddy heading for the kitchen, the tips of his walker thundering on the rugless plank floor. He turned, huffing, and leaned into his walker. He stared at Sullivan's hands, which were rapidly making and unmaking fists.

"There's some wood in the shed," Freddy said, "but it's wet. We'll have to get some from the barn on the hill. I'll go."

"Need a hand?" Sullivan said. "Well, I mean, maybe you could stay here and keep an eye on things."

Freddy kept looking at Sullivan's fists.

Natalie reappeared, towing a rug. She slapped the snow from her coat. Marian, striding cheerfully, was on her way out the door with Freddy. Sullivan unsnapped Freddy's guitar case—it was a top-of-the-line Martin—and blew on the strings; his breath billowed in small, swift clouds.

"Cold sharps the strings." Sullivan strummed with his gloves on. "Heat flats them. Simple physics."

"No shit, Sherlock," Natalie said. Her hair tumbled out of her cap. She winged her arms behind her head, but there was still not enough hair to make a braid. She kept tugging, exposing the roots.

"Where'd they go?" she asked.

"Firewood." He spread the rug. Snow was melting in his socks.

Natalie winked, then laughed, her eyes crossing. She sat by the hearth and began to sing about a child and a cauliflower in the accentless French Sullivan envied. She kept time by knocking her boot on the hearth. She stopped singing almost immediately, but kept tapping.

"I had three miscarriages in India."

"Three? Freddy told me about one."

"Three." She spread her fingers in front of her face, still tapping, still the song. "I thought everybody knew that about me. The doctor says I'm young, I should keep trying. But my body doesn't always listen when I tell it what to do." She silenced her boot. "You don't have that problem, do you?"

"No." Sullivan felt they shared a talent for renunciation.

"I should hope not. Simple physics, right?"

Squirrels scrambled in the attic: they looked up. Natalie leaned forward, shoving the heel of her hand into her cheek, forcing herself to lisp. "You going to get busy about the war again?" She was still inspecting the ceiling.

"What war?"

Natalie did not smile. "College kids are burning their draft cards. *Kids,* for chrissake. Robert Lowell, Norman Mailer, even what's-their-name, those Jesuit twins . . ."

"They're not twins, they're brothers. And only one of them's a Jesuit. His Eminence is keeping an eye on me."

"So what?"

He blushed, realizing he'd also suggested "keeping an eye on things" to Freddy.

"So fucking what?" Natalie said. "I'm dipping candles for the Quakers."

"So I'm waiting."

"Obedience—that's all you priests ever worry about. You're such a conceited bunch of slaves. Are you aware that two monks have already torched themselves in Saigon?" She held two fingers in front of her face.

"What should I care what you think about priests? At least I was of some real use in India. What do you want from me?"

"Everything."

Marian stepped inside. "I heard you singing."

She sat down opposite Sullivan, who took a while tuning the guitar. Natalie stood up and straightened the Polo Grounds picture. Marian adjusted her jeans and smiled at Sullivan as she opened her coat, unveiling a red sweater illustrated with a reindeer and stylized snowflakes. Natalie sat down and began singing. Sullivan found her in E flat and strummed a few changes, gradually picking up the resiny scent of Marian's hair, which he focused on without looking at her, the way he might imagine a word.

Freddy swiveled his walker acrobatically, kicked the door shut. Snow slid with a washboard noise from the eaves.

"You got to go for a walk on that hill," he said. "It's fantastic." He trundled to the fireplace and dumped three logs out of his coat. Natalie pulled in her legs as they fell.

"Anybody got a match?" Sullivan asked.

"Me," Marian said. "I do."

Sullivan stacked the logs, stuffed trash under them and screwed some newspapers. When he finally got one of Marian's wooden matches to strike—why *wooden* matches?—the whole box flared up, crisping the hairs on the back of his hand in the shape of tiny ferns. He backed away from the fire. Natalie and Freddy sorted twigs. The room flickered. Sullivan felt heat on his cheeks, sulfur dissolving in his nose. Marian accompanied him to the doorway.

In the center of the fireplace, an empty milk carton

stood straight up, seemingly untouched, its wax coat hissing while the sides and back panels caught fire and thin flames beat around the base. The front panel, just a bit farther from the kindling, remained intact, a martyr ecstatic at the stake, body melting around bones, a song one of them was supposed to sing.

They walked toward the back porch, spiked with young icicles, and past the old hand pump, where Marian fell. She bounced right back up, snow bearding her cheeks.

The hill was a steep pasture just beginning to grow in, a few low firs poking through the snow, which fell now in fat, windless flakes. The hill, the shrubs, the low clouds—they were all the same: everything illuminated as if from within, shadowless. In deference to the whiteness of it all, they did not speak for several minutes.

"That's some imagination you got, Sister," Sullivan said finally. "What was all that malarkey about Radcliffe?"

"Do you think you can get what you want by doing what you're supposed to do?" she said.

He sniffled and trudged uphill.

"*I* don't think you can." She nibbled snow from her mitten. "I used to think so, but not anymore. I'd like to be like Natalie. I'd like to be someone like her. She's an idealist and she lives in the country. I'd like to be able to do the things she does. But it seems like more than I could handle, teaching and taking courses and working politically and taking care of Freddy and thinking about raising a family. And she really is a lovely person. I admire her. She cares so freely."

Stray sleet ticked on their clothes.

"You're already teaching school and raising kids."

"Yeah, but they're not my own. I mean, I'm not sorry I did it, going into the convent. I mean I'm really crazy about the kids. The only thing I can't stand is when they fight." She punched her mittens together. "And they fight so much. I'm not leaving the order unless I feel I have to have a kid of my own. I don't miss having a kid, but I get depressed. It's like I miss being born myself or something."

"I like being a priest. It's great until they start doing that rabbit's-foot number on you. Most people don't talk to you, they talk to the suit."

Her gaze was bright on him. "I did a lot of sewing last night. I sewed patches on my jeans, two of them, and I moved a button on my khaki shirt. Then I dreamed about buying hundred-dollar boots." She made a circle with her thumb and forefinger: perfection.

He laughed. "Hundred-dollar boots are a war crime, Sister."

"Well, you know what they say: you can take the nun out of California, but you can't take the California out of the nun."

She swept snow off a rock and sat down, planting her hands behind her.

"I like you," he said.

"Why?"

"Well. Well, because you're a good person."

Marian chewed her mitten. "Oh, n-n-n-no, no, no! You'd like me a lot better if I were Natalie, wouldn't you? Why don't you just say so?"

He was distracted by a sudden swirling of snow and sleet. The wind began repeating the same word: *slow-cold, slowcold.* They collided; she pulled away, suppressing a gasp. Below them, veiled in the storm, the house was a toy. Peach-colored sparks spat from the chimney. Sullivan thought he heard them snapping as he knelt down.

"Maybe I should drop some acid," she said.

"Drugs are a disappointment, Sister. Drugs are *about* disappointment."

"Oh yeah? Aren't you disappointed? Don't you ever get mad?"

"No. Mostly it feels like a dime in my shoes, sex does. Drugs are a parody of need."

"I wasn't talking about sex. And whose need are you talking about, for crying out loud?"

"Mine, I guess."

When he touched her, the back of his hand against her throat, she looked serious, almost stern. She slid off the rock and knelt facing him.

"There's something I've been wanting to ask you," he said.

"What?" Marian closed her eyes, stuck out her tongue and tasted the snowflakes.

"Do nuns have hair?" he said.

She opened her eyes. "Do cowboys have hair?"

"Cowboys always wear their cowboy hats." He kissed the hollow of her neck and moved his mouth to her chin.

"Nuns always wear their nun outfits," she said, "even in the shower. Nuns squint."

"Cowboys squint." He risked her breasts. She guided his hand to her belt buckle. The belt was wampum and leather, something one of her kids must have made. "Cowboys court the weather and beat up on women," he continued. "Cowboys don't give a hoot. Cowboys have blue eyes in brown faces."

She was easing her jeans down her hips. He opened his coat and tented it over their shoulders.

"Nuns have brown eyes in blue faces." She slid out of her pants with a double motion, separated by a sigh that was pleasured and impatient at the same time.

"Nuns fight," she said. "Nuns don't have any money."

"Cowboys always sit in the shade," he said. "Cowboys stink, cowboys drink, cowboys fight, cowboys remember the good old days."

She pulled her sweater up, the reindeer dancing away. He craned his head and sucked her right nipple, the color of an apricot. Her breasts were small and wall-eyed, incredibly warm. She leaned back, letting her hair scatter on the snow. He felt a slight breeze.

She spread her fingers, forking his cock. He was in her, soft at first, a little bundle. He was shocked at how warm she was. Then he forgot the cold, there was no cold, her warmth spread to him. He closed his eyes, needing blindness to prolong the pleasure. He ejaculated. Most of the semen spilled out, glistening, viscous on her thighs, a new species of snow.

"Now you know," she said. "Nuns really don't have hair."

"Where's the blood? There's no blood."

Marian braced herself on her elbows. "I don't have my period or anything."

"Yeah, but . . ."

Marian pulled up her pants and lay back on her side.

"There was this old shale quarry where we used to go skinny-dipping," she said. "There were three guys who always hiked to the top and dove off. There was a whole family that used to swim at one end. There were two girls, sisters about twelve or thirteen. Budding breasts, no hips. There was a boy who used to come by himself, a farm kid with a slouch and a sunburned neck. He always, I mean he *always* had a huge erection that bobbed up and down like a diving board. And there was Roger. He owned the quarry and he was rich. He always had a six-pack cooling in the water. He told me that in California all the aborigines had been nudists. Whenever I went there, Roger offered me his spot on the flattest rock. You know what an aborigine is?"

"The first one?" Sullivan swallowed.

"Right. Roger was my aborigine. We used to spend afternoons calculating how deep the quarry was by dropping rocks and listening for clicks. About sixty feet, we figured. People around Riverside kept on saying the quarry was bottomless. People like to make mysteries out of the stupidest things."

"What stupidest things?"

"Deep things." Marian laughed.

Sullivan still felt warm, though snow was running down his neck. They rested. After a while, this didn't seem right. He walked toward a shed halfway down the hill. Marian got up but didn't follow.

The shed stank of kerosene, rotten leaves and rat shit, the unresolved odors of a young ruin. A bird whose call was like water spilling rapidly from a tiny bottle fluttered out of its nest. Sullivan's eyes swarmed over the snapped-off hay rakes and strangled cards of baling twine and staveless barrels and labelless cans speckled with condensation. He didn't see what he wanted. He made an effort to focus.

He felt the ax before he saw it. He felt the shape of

the handle, not quite straight, not quite curved, a serpent tensing under his boot. He grabbed it before it
turned on him.

There wasn't much of a back wall to the shed. Sullivan headed uphill, away from Marian. He stumbled.
He pulled his boot out of the snow, pushed the other
one ahead just fast enough to keep from falling. He
stumbled again, drawn to the ground.

"Hey, what are you doing?" Marian's voice carried
easily.

Firewood. He wanted a tree, of course.

"Hey, wait up," Marian called. "I'm out of breath."
She was a distant smudge in the snow.

He followed the indented ribbon of a game trail to a
row of pines. Sullivan took his first swing on the run,
missing the trunk completely. He must have been moving fast. The snapping of the branches called him back,
told him he'd do better if he planted his feet. He swung
again without control. The ax slithered. He swung
again. The tree was little more than a sapling; it
wouldn't stand still. He aimed lower, just above the
roots, where the trunk couldn't sponge the blows. The
wood was slippery and green, bark skinned away,
flayed into strips, and he saw this was going to be a
matter of battering the tree down rather than severing
it chip by chip. The ax shuddered. He stomped his boot
against the trunk until it began to give.

"Hey, cut it out," Marian said. "You're frightening
me."

He gave the trunk a final kick and snapped it off. It
bled aromatically. How Anglo-Saxon it was to feel
guilty about flowers, he thought.

He stood perfectly still for several minutes after
Marian ran back to the house. The more he studied the

stump and the sap beading on the flung-off chips, the slower his breathing became.

He lay down and looked into the clouds and let the flakes fall into his eyes, forcing himself not to blink. His eyes seemed to be the only organs capable of registering the cold: they stung. He shut them tight. He opened them immediately, intending to welcome the snowflakes again. They jabbed at his eyes like insects. He herded the clouds: Delhi, Bengal, Bombay. Delhi, Bengal, Bombay, Monsoon.

Nothing touch.

Except her. And her without a single snake of experience in her eyes.

Every time Sullivan went out back to pee, the drifts were deeper. There was plenty of beer. He also drank half a bottle of wine, some brandy and a pot of tea. The fire grew old, heavy-lidded; flames sleeved the logs.

Marian was making more tea. Upstairs, Natalie and Freddy were having a pillow fight, their shouts floating like small voices from a radio. Marian tossed a tea bag at the fire. It missed, hit the bricks on the side, stuck for a second like a clumsy dance hesitation, then sucked away and plopped on the hearth, hissing. Sullivan propped his feet against the fireplace. His shoes were soaked, he was shivering and there was a sharp pain in his left foot. Marian napped with her back to him.

Sparks popped from a sappy log. It was a lovers' fire, a liars' fire. It was a tribute to the infinite species of smoke. It was possible, of course, to discern definite patterns. Definite patterns.

The small of her back flickered, blue and orange. Her

buttocks quivered, then subsided, as if she were running in a dream.

The last log was silhouetted in front of its own flame. They made love again, slowly. He was becoming younger and wiser.

The Land Rover started right up but the headlights wouldn't work. Freddy employed one of Natalie's bobby pins for a fuse. Every few miles they had to stop and put a new one in before the wiring melted, and when Natalie's bobby pins ran out, they started in on Marian's, and before they were halfway to the city, the women's hair was flying and Freddy was braying Gilbert and Sullivan. The slush steamed in a light rain.

The animal came out of darkness and rain as if it had been thrown at the car.

"Oh my God," Natalie said.

Sullivan had time to remember she'd used the same offhand tone of sudden illumination when they crashed in India. He looked up to see something large and alive disappear, head and tail seesawing, over the top of the windshield. He felt sympathetically airborne.

Freddy hit the brakes; the wheels locked and the Land Rover wobbled onto the shoulder.

"A deer," Freddy said.

The carcass came to rest on the snowbank behind them. It was a mature doe. She lay flat on her side, as if laid out on a table, unable to move a muscle, a pale red blot seeping across her flank. What remained of her life retreated to the rapid rise and fall of her chest and shimmered in the white panic rim around her eye. Up close, her legs crumpled, she didn't look much like

Bambi: she had the eye of a cow, the head of a large rodent.

"It's suffering," Natalie said. The sleet pelted them. Freddy leaned out the window, yanked off his glove with his teeth and drummed the door.

"Do we have to report it or something?" Marian said.

"Anybody got a knife?" Sullivan said.

"Here," Freddy said. "There's one in here somewhere."

"It's still suffering," Natalie said.

Freddy waved his Swiss Army knife. He pointed at the hood, which seemed to have been dented out of proportion to the weight of the doe.

"What a mess," he said. "Which blade do you want?" He began picking at the side of the knife, but opening it was something he could no longer accomplish.

Sullivan pried out the largest blade, no more than an inch and a half long. The knife and the doe were a collusion of miniatures.

The doe's eye rolled away from Sullivan when he knelt at her shoulder. His ankle tingled. He shifted in an attempt to shake the sensation. It persisted. The blade was dull; it would not pierce the wet, matted coat.

"It's all right," Marian was saying to the doe. "It's all right."

It was impossible to tell what animals were thinking; their gestures were too operatic. Sullivan punctured the doe's neck. There was a sound of canvas tearing. The blood came freely, pooling on ice blackened by passing cars, horns bleating shamelessly. He stayed on his knees till the doe's eye relaxed into a gaze that looked beyond him. A plow came by, tooting, burying her hindquarters with slush. Marian brushed her off.

Natalie took the occasion to empty the ashtray. "It's

so lucky we had you with us, Father," she said in
French, translating immediately for Marian.

"Torna, non ti scorda da me . . ."
Nunzio's song and the glugging of hair tonic show-
ered Peanuts' scalp. Nunzio, the barber, pampered his
potbelly and played the banjo, which he called, in comparison to his voice, "a plunky instrument." Peanuts
had seen him slip into his Roadmaster and fold a towel
across his belly so the steering wheel wouldn't wear a
groove in the blazer he wore to the track. Peanuts
trusted him. Nunzio trusted only food and babies.
". . . core 'ingrato . . ." Nunzio bowed. "That's some
gorgeous head of hair you got on you, kid. Ooooh!
Makes all the girls crazy, right? You lucky dog, you."
Peanuts didn't think he was such a lucky dog.
"You know what I call this haircut?" Nunzio pinched
his cheek. "I call this haircut the Crime Wave."
Nunzio bowed again, kept clipping and singing along
with his Dago dry-hump records. He checked out the
girls passing his window.
Peanuts paid Nunzio a dollar and his father tipped
him another half a buck and gave Peanuts a nickel for
the weight-and-fate machine that stood glimmering by
the door, an elegantly mirrored musical instrument.
85 lbs. You Are Lucky In Love.
Peanuts understood from his father's generosity and
silence that Grandpa Duke must have taken a turn for
the worse.

———

There had always been someone in Peanuts' family called Duke. The name Duke—in a family with names as plain as potatoes: Jim, Mike, Jack—was a tip of the hat, a pat on the back, now and then a sly twist of the arm, a title sometimes applied to Peanuts, as in "How 'bout taking out the garbage once in a while, Duke?" but belonging properly to his grandfather, Duke Farrell, his mother's father, who'd been known as Duke and nothing else since retiring from the Transit Authority the day before Peanuts was baptized. Deep in his seventies, Duke Farrell still played the accordion like a magician.

Back home from Nunzio's, Peanuts passed his hand over the wallpaper in the foyer. The neatness of the living room stared at him. He walked by the sunset painting, the umbrella stand that always stood empty, blue shadows, African violets, a lonely ball of orange lint and the life-size Sacred Heart pierced by a tin sword. In every room a clock was ticking. His mother was in the kitchen.

"Why don't you just sit down for a minute, Denny," she said, neglecting to kiss him.

He heard a sound familiar from *Gunsmoke:* clattering of cornstalks followed by distant screeching: crows in a crow-filled sky. His father was making room for his coat in the closet, shoving the metal hangers around.

"The Duke's upstairs," he said. "He wants to see you, Denny. Don't contradict him. He doesn't know what he's saying anymore."

"Says who?" his mother said. "He's not conked out yet." She looked up swiftly, a glass bell struck in her heart. She ran to Peanuts and grabbed him by the shoulders and whispered fiercely, her grief thawing to a single cool tear: "Tell Grandpa you love him, Denny." Then she broke away and began to dust the *Encyclopedia Americana.*

"Cheer him up." His father took his hand. "Tell him I got a hot date for him this evening."

Duke's skin looked like paper on which spots of water had dried. His eyes were open, milky, staring straight ahead. Between his nose and his upper lip, a strand of bloody snot was glistening. The only sound Peanuts could hear was the whistling of Duke's breath. He lowered himself on the edge of the bed, keeping some of his weight on the floor in case he had to get up in a hurry. He thought for a moment the clock had stopped. He exhaled. The ticking returned.

There'd been a day, not so long ago, when a hot date wasn't beyond the Duke. It was said of Peanuts' grandfather that, early on, he had renounced all earthly ambitions except drinking and fooling around, meaning women. "I don't really mind," his mother had said, "but I do mind when he parks them right in front of the house," referring to the lady friends in Duke's Coupe de Ville.

But this past year, since his stroke, he just sat around, drank a bit, old and useless and happy as stained upholstery, the only sloppy thing tolerated in the house. His daughter, Peanuts' mother, kept after him to take a bath. She told him he was getting to smell like the Gowanus Canal. Peanuts wondered what the Gowanus Canal smelled like. "Its stink could stun small animals," Duke bragged, "and cause the eyes of primates to tear." The bowls of his pipes were stained and cracked and so were the teeth that clenched the stems. He had an arsenal of flashlights to guide him through familiar places that had become forbidding and he had a colossal collection of hats. He could no longer read Murray Kempton, but he liked talking back to the television.

"Get me a Kleenex, will you, kid?"

Peanuts hopped up.

"Thanks, kid." Duke's voice was relaxed, his eyes were still closed. "You got a comb on you?"

Peanuts shrugged and ran his hands through his curls. Duke's eyes opened and closed like slow fans. He hoisted himself up on his elbows. Peanuts plumped the pillows. Duke sniffled, the blood welling brightly in his nostrils.

"It's a shame I never got to see you serving Mass," Duke said. "Or saying the Latin. They tell me you do it well."

"Gloria in excelsis Deo," Peanuts said. "Et in terra pax hominibus bonae voluntatis. Laudamas te. Benedicimus te. Adoramus te. Glorificamus te. Gratias agimus tibi propter magnam gloriam tuam. Domine Deus, rex caelestis, Deus pater omnipotens. Domine filii unigenite, Jesu Christe. Domine Deus, agnus Dei, Filius Patris. Qui tollis peccata mundi, suscipe deprecationem nostram. Qui sedes ad dexteram Patris, miserere nobis. Quoniam tu solus sanctus, tu solus Dominus, tu solus altissimus, Jesu Christe. Cum sancto spiritu in gloria Dei Patris, Amen."

Duke's lips parted in astonishment, disclosing his pale green tongue. Peanuts fell against his grandfather's chest and blotted his tears on the shirt of his pajamas, remembering:

Duke is wearing his plaid jacket, plaid pants and plaid vest. Bright reds and yellows. What does it matter the plaid's a Scottish tartan? It's his birthday, he's Irish. We are taking him to the Casablanca Inn for steak and the waiters are going to sing to him over pink cake sprouting candles. Oh yes, he is wearing white socks. How we love our white socks. Duke takes his seat. We wait for drinks. Duke flaps a pack of sugar so that it will settle to one side before he opens it. This goes on for four or five minutes. Then Peanuts' father asks Duke what the fuck he thinks he's doing and his mother puts her hand on Duke's to keep him down.

Downstairs in the kitchen, Peanuts poured himself a glass of milk. The house seemed undressed by grief.

His mother was washing the dishes. His father sat at the table fondling his tumbler of whiskey. His mother stacked the last plate. The gas flame flapped when she turned the stove on. She brewed some tea and sucked it over the brim with a sound which if magnified would have been the rattling of a stick along a picket fence. This usually aggravated Peanuts' father, but now he paid no attention.

His mother heated more water and poured it in two pails, adding Epsom salts. She sat at the table and leaned on her elbows. She dunked one foot, then the other in the steaming pails, sighing.

"Should I call my brother, Jim?" she said.

"Wait," his father said. "I'll call him in a minute."

His mother stared at the phone. "You got to be a mind reader around here. Nobody says anything."

"I'll *call* him, Grace."

Peanuts added water, hot by mistake, to a can of orange juice concentrate.

"Be sure to turn the faucet all the way off," his mother said. "Last night it was dripping so much I thought it would drive me nuts. I could hear it all the way upstairs. I said to myself, if it drips once more, I'm going to get up and fix the damn thing, and that's when it stopped dripping, wouldn't you know."

It occurred to Peanuts that his mother was saying exactly what was on her mind, no more, no less. He wrapped his arms around her. She was very warm, damp, on the brink of sweating. Her hair, as he looked down at it, was thin and gray. She turned her face to him slowly, like a planet showing a section of her surface to the sun. He remembered her once looking at his father like that.

Seven

"Twelve people!" Father Sullivan said. "What kind of turnout is twelve people, Monroe? I brought a whole box of books for twelve people?"

"What can I tell you?" Dr. Silberman said, squeezing his bow tie. "I'm sorry for the size of the turnout. But so what? Anyplace else, you get a hundred people, ninety-five of them are Feds. Here at least you got a hundred percent revolutionaries. Like the twelve apostles, right?"

Sullivan, decked out in his tropical cassock, winced cordially.

The Young Spartacists weren't so young anymore. The hall smelled like a European train: there were several cigars and several hand-knit sweaters tucked under belts, and right behind him, a man wearing red earmuffs was pointing out that of all the Marxists, Trotsky had the largest soul because he, Trotsky, had predicted that one day the average human being, the ordinary Joe, would rise to the heights of an Aristotle, a Goethe, an Alexander Berkman, to which his friend,

who was pacing up and down with a sort of belly-
forward glide, the way a wasp flies, replied that it was
a scientific fact that an anarchist like Berkman could
never shoot straight at an oligarch like Frick because
no matter how many shots he fired, he'd always be a
schmuck for going up against such a highly organized
state apparatus in the first place.

Sullivan took a bite out of his baloney sandwich and
wondered why he felt all these people were so full of
shit. The reasons, of course, were numberless. He was
no longer a judge of such things. The truth was that one
thing and one thing only inhabited Sullivan's mind and
it was no longer in his power to exclude it: Marian's
thighs, through which he'd listened to her whole body
when they made love in Sister Carmela's, the ex-Sister
Superior's brownstone last night, moonlight lacing
their legs. During orgasm, she informed him, the sense
of smell was the last to leave and the first to return.
They were in the chafed-chin stage of infatuation. They
got to sleep at four-thirty, liquefied on the reeking
sheets. Her rosary crashed on the table glass.

Dr. Silberman, in the present tense, tapped a cigarette on his silver case. He was running interference
for the philosopher in red earmuffs, who wanted to get
Sullivan's views about Einstein's *dime und spaze*.

"By the way, Jack," Silberman said, "I got some
press coverage also. See over there? That's what's-his-
name from the whaddayacallit News Service."

"Oh brother," Sullivan said. "Not McSweeney."

"Be glad he's here. We don't usually let non-mem-
bers into these meetings."

"I know him from Fordham. He sends me Christmas
cards. He's a cop, Monroe."

"Jewish people don't get regular Christmas cards; we

get pictures of giraffes and things. What do you expect?"

McSweeney waved with the tips of his fingers and opened a bosomy paperback, cracking its spine. With the book, he looked a little off, like a farmer carrying a watering can. At Fordham he'd been a phenomenal shot-putter and javelin-hurler, though the fatal accident involving his coach cast a pall on his intercollegiate career. His shoes were bargelike, his limbs homeless. His grin was the result of a pushed button.

Marian, standing in the doorway, smiled behind the mitten in her mouth. Her shoulder-bag strap separated her breasts.

"Hiya Father. Hi Dr. Silberman. It's freezing in here." She kissed Sullivan dryly and hiccuped.

"Glad you could make it," Silberman said.

"Me too," she said. "We need more Catholic politicians."

She poured herself a cup of water at the lectern. She gulped it down, poured another, gulped that one, hiccuped, wiped her mouth and exhaled. "I mean just as we need more Catholic engineers, more Catholic baseball players, more Catholic television personalities . . ." She poured another cup of water.

"She's a nice girl, Jack." Silberman towed Sullivan toward the lectern. "Never trust nice."

Silberman folded his brow and called for order. "Friends, comrades. Maybe some of you have seen our guest speaker on a previous occasion. Maybe some of you saw him at the Mobilization March in front of the UN last month. Maybe you saw him getting arrested in front of St. Patrick's earlier this year. He was the Irishman in the white uniform . . ."

This was Sullivan's first experience as an eccentric

on display. He wriggled as if controlling an itch.
McSweeney marked his place with a paper clip.
Marian was looking around and feeling better.

"So it's my great personal pleasure to introduce if I
may at this time Father Jack Sullivan, a friend and a
patient of mine I might add who brings with him in
addition to his many other literary and political and
dental credentials the personal warm salutations of
the chairman of the Revolutionary League of the State
of Bihar which needless to say is in India—am I right
about that, Jack?—where he recently completed an
extended stay and is now back with us to take up his
part in the struggle to dismantle the oligarchy and the
state war machine. Thank you. Father Jack."

The Spartacists' applause was skimpy, but it startled
Sullivan, tranced again. The Spartacists were gathered
in knots of two or three, sitting in chairs that were
strewn around the loft rather than arranged in rows.
They folded their arms like men who'd spent a lifetime
waiting for the impossible, waiting to be persuaded.

Sullivan stepped back and slipped a notebook out of
his cassock. Marian pinched her finger trying to get a
grip on one of the folding chairs. Unexpectedly, Sullivan's notebook started to shiver.

He got through two new sonnets and a translation
from Tagore. Marian and Silberman held their heads,
apparently thinking very hard, in tandem. Sullivan
squinted through the layer of cigar smoke that had
settled at eye level. He was not able to continue without trembling. There was not a drop left in the pitcher
Marian had drained. The Spartacists appeared baffled
but pleased, like men witnessing a knot-tying demonstration. McSweeney squeezed the paperback between
his knees.

"Okay, if there's any questions . . ." Sullivan said.

"So you claim to have been arrested." The questioner stood up and clasped his hands behind his back. "What were the charges?"

"Disturbing the peace," Sullivan said. "We were calling attention to the Cardinal's support of the disturbance of the peace in Vietnam. His Eminence called the cops because we were disturbing his peace outside St. Patrick's."

"We?" the man said. "What we? Who's this we?"

"Clergy Concerned About the War in Vietnam. His Eminence has also instructed me to say nothing more on the subject of the war, lest we disturb his peace even further. I am obliged to some extent to honor his Eminence's request. That is, so long as I'm in his diocese."

"So leave."

The man sat down to brisk applause. Sullivan waited. His trembling subsided.

Silberman cleared his throat. "Excuse me, Father Jack, but Ernst Mandel, a leading theorist of the Fourth International, maintains, and I quote, that the major part of American capital exports have been invested in other imperialist countries, and that this does not contradict the classical Marxist analysis."

Sullivan folded his arms.

"Would you agree, then, Father, that a capitalist system could behave decently in the international economy, or is it forever fated to do evil?"

Applause. Marian hiccuped.

"Fated to do evil?" Sullivan said. "Is that the question?"

"Yes, but not in the sentimental bourgeois sense."

Silberman descended breathlessly into his chair.

"Yes," Sullivan said. "Well. We do live in a country

where thieves predict the future. But we can always
hope with St. Augustine that God makes good use of
sin."

"Sin!" The guy with red earmuffs bolted to his feet.
"What is this—the Salvation Army?"

Four of the Spartacists started to walk out, abusing
the legs of chairs on their way. Silberman stood up.

"We were speaking of Ernst Mandel, Father, and the
deflection of capital from the Third World. We were
speaking of the Third World . . ."

"Yes, the Third World, the Third World. Excuse me."
Sullivan trapped a sneeze. "Yes, Christianity and Com-
munism . . ."

"Communists!" The man hurled his earmuffs at Sullivan. His eyes were flies, furious in a web. "What are
you talking about Communists? What is this red-
baiting?"

"Red-baiting?" Sullivan threw the earmuffs back.
"Red-baiting? I'm the Communist here."

Sullivan retrieved the baloney sandwich from his
pocket and slapped it on the lectern. He dug out a
five-dollar bill. He pushed the sandwich to one side,
held up the bill and flicked it. The Spartacists paused
in the doorway. He gripped the money and raised it
over his head.

"Okay," he said. "This is bread."

He lowered the bill and genuflected, then elevated
the sandwich the same as the money.

"This is my body," he said.

Marian hiccuped, dropping her gum in her lap.

McSweeney scrubbed his face like an enormous
blond fly.

———

Silberman took them to Ratner's. The waiter poured water in fingerprinted glasses and went back to his newspaper. Marian and Sullivan held hands under the table. Marian drank everyone's water and chewed the ice.

"You know what I believe?" Silberman said. "I believe everybody's got a soul just like his hands."

He clapped his hands sharply. The waiter jumped, rattling his paper.

"Thirty, thirty-five years ago," Silberman said, "this joint was full of revolutionaries, right? Not a bunch of disaffected English-major blobs like you got today. Listen." He clapped his hands again. "We used to think hands clapping was cannons."

"You were right, Monroe." Something fell into Sullivan's eye.

"Stop. You're going to make an old man brech. I was wrong."

"I thought it was a wonderful evening," Marian said.

Silberman eyed Sullivan. "You know what a luft-mensch is? I'll tell you. It's someone who lives on—on God knows what—on air."

"Actually," Marian said, "I've heard such people really do exist. In the Far East, and in California maybe, too."

They caught the F train back to Brooklyn. Sullivan dozed and had a noisy dream about Natalie drawing him a map of the Rajasthan desert, including nonexistent intersections. SPOTLIGHT, she writes in several places. Sullivan takes the pencil from her hand and sketches the route from the mission to Jaipur, to Delhi, and then Natalie takes the pencil and erases the road.

She smiles sadly at him, signifying she is dead. "You can erase the line," she says. "But you can't erase the impression."

He was awakened at Charyn Street by warm tears dropping on his wrist. He thought at first they might be Natalie's, and he was relieved to know she was still alive. He did not open his eyes until he heard a strange sigh.

Marian was unstringing a stalk of celery from Ratner's. Torsos tilted; the doors wheezed open.

"I'm pregnant, Jack."

He immediately admired the neatness of her revenge.

"at thE buckSkin bar wEdnESday wEt tEEShirt contESt thurSday bill & zaza high StEpping dancE tEam tonight livE muSic & dancing two guyS from vEgaS mErry xmaS."

"Please stop walking like you're not with me," Sister Marian said.

"Excuse me," Father Sullivan said.

They stood in the drizzle long enough to figure out what the problem with the sign was, aside from the seasonal greeting, which was six weeks out of date. The Casablanca Inn, featuring the Buckskin Bar, was situated on Third Avenue between Brooklyn Vacuum Service and Sundaze, a boutique. There was a NO BARE FEET sign in the window, meaning they didn't cater to college boys. Con Ed steam cast a shadow darker than itself on the slush.

The drizzle forced Sullivan to look down.

"What's that?" Marian said.

"Somebody's tooth."

He put the tooth in his pocket, then changed his mind and tossed it away with his cigarette, which landed in a puddle and gave a capillary hiss, smoke clinging to the water like a veil.

A hairy dog was leashed outside. He yapped at Marian. She touched him under his chin.

"If you were obedient, you wouldn't be tied up," she said. "But you're not, so you are."

The bar had spools of flypaper, a revolving Schaefer sign with bubbles and a clock, trailing plastic geraniums, an autographed glossy of Hugh Downs, a poster for a charter tour of Ireland and Lourdes led by a handsome Monsignor, and a rare photo of Rocky Marciano on all fours. Two musicians, resigned to another medley of old favorites, were setting up.

"Hiya, Jack," Roz said. Her beehive jiggled, her eyelashes jiggled, her cigarette jiggled. "Whaddaya say?"

"How're you feeling, dear?" Sullivan said. "What's the special today?"

"I got nice lobster."

"Lovely."

The musicians struck up something that might have been a polka. A man at the bar removed his hat and did Jimmy Durante.

"Can I have two grilled cheese sandwiches please?" Marian said.

"Anything to drink with that, dearie?" Roz said.

Sullivan asked what kind of wine there was.

"Red and white."

"Couple of Schaefers," he said.

Roz patted Marian's cheek. "Don't worry, dearie. It's just like a D-and-C. Better days are coming."

The "clinic" was in a motel just on the Jersey side of the Holland Tunnel. *Motel,* Sister Marian thought. The word itself had a broken heart.

The room felt cramped and aimlessly frantic, like a bus terminal. Jack was not permitted to stay. There were six other women in the . . . well, office, Marian supposed it was, all black or Puerto Rican. On a table next to the reception desk, a black-and-white TV was tuned to *American Bandstand:* Dick Clark looked puffy. Marian caught herself wondering how his toupee would taste.

Two men appeared and talked briefly with the receptionist, who shook her head to everything they said and kept typing. One, a tall black man with a shock of white in his hair, stuffed a roll of tens and twenties in his pocket. Why? He examined file cards and took money from the youngest-looking woman, a teenager with a cross around her neck and a stuffed pink animal in her lap. One woman dozed. Another chewed gum. Those Puerto Ricans with their everlasting gum. Two of them, looking at everything but each other, carried on a bored conversation about landlords. The poor were bored with their troubles, the rich with their pleasures. She'd try to remember that for Jack. Only it wasn't boredom. It was the numb alertness of prisoners. The teenager nodded, eager only for her turn to pass. Why? Marian was thirsty.

The other man, who was white and wore his sport

jacket buttoned at the bottom button, asked her the date of her last period.

"December twenty-fourth," she said. She meant January twenty-fourth. But before she could correct herself, the man said, "Sorry," and lifted her by the elbow.

"Wait a minute," the black man said. "I'll handle this."

The white man dropped her elbow.

"January twenty-fourth," Marian squeaked. "January twenty-fourth. January twenty-fourth."

"Okay," the black man said. "Now, do *you* have any questions?" He had incredibly long eyelashes. He smiled without looking at her, exactly the opposite of what a priest would do: look at her without smiling, always make her feel bad for doing something wrong. Oh, that reprobate, the phony, that mule.

"No questions," she answered, forcing herself to breathe through her nose. She took the three hundred-dollar bills, still chilly from the outside air, out of her purse. She loved the snapping of fresh paper money and the happy weight of Kennedy half-dollars.

An Indian woman in a doctorish white coat called the teenager. She steered the girl toward a green-glass door, then turned to Marian and said, "Come on, now. You too."

In a room without chairs, the Indian woman briefed them about "the procedure." The teenager confided that she took the pill sometimes.

"Well, this is like strong menstrual cramps." The Indian woman was controlling a sudden interest in her fingernails. "Maybe not even that. Now we will practice breathing in slowly through our noses and then through our mouths. Vice versa is okey-dokey too, if you prefer."

The teenager looked at Marian and copied what she did until finally the Indian woman led her out. Alone, Marian saw that the room was just like any other gynecological examining room. There was a table with knee holders instead of stirrups, and on the floor a porcelain bowl with a chip the shape of a butterfly. Beautiful. The white man came in. He had replaced his sport jacket with a smock.

"Undress, please, from the waist down." His smile was breathy, assured. He had vertical lines on his forehead. "Sit all the way down at the end of the table. All the way."

He pulled her forward.

"Lie back, that's right. Relax. Legs up."

The speculum was colder, colder than her coins. She inhaled and held her breath as he dilated her. She listened to the wheels of his rolling chair, chasing her pain, and exhaled in small, slow bursts. She clenched and unclenched her fist, as Sister Superior had done showing her tattooed heart. A heart with a what? A knife? A baby? A heart with another heart? It was impossible.

His chair rolled back. His flashlight clicked.

"You're Dr. Jimmy's patient?" He sighed. "From my pelvic examination you do not appear to be pregnant. However . . ."

He hooked the machine into her uterus.

"This will pinch a little bit. I'm just inserting the tube. The whole procedure will last thirty to forty-five seconds."

A sound like a small cement mixer. Suction. She remembered Natalie's advice: "You think if it goes on for another second, you'll die. Then it's over."

Brief respite. Heart escaping to her throat. Suction

again. She was gasping and groaning. She told the
fetus: I'm sorry, you can't have my body. The baby's
soul filled the room. It was a female.

"Breathe deeply. Deeply, now."

Why?

Over. Then it's over.

"From what I can see, you were not pregnant." He
left the room. The Indian woman returned. Marian's
right shoulder was buzzing.

"Can you sit up? Give me your hands."

She felt herself being tugged upright.

"You made it all up," the nurse said. "It was all in
your head. Are you seeing black spots in front of your
eyes? You weren't even pregnant, see that? The nervous system, that is the worst system in the whole body
all right."

She popped an amyl nitrate under Marian's nose and
fanned the fumes toward her. Marian felt that if she
fainted now she wouldn't regain consciousness.

"Come on now. You go lie down in the bed. You made
the whole thing up."

Marian saw four cots under a row of windows without shades. She was not aware of walking to another
room. No, five cots. Six.

"Lie in the bed. No, there."

Marian stumbled into one of the cots, too weak to
pull the blanket out from under herself. She was unable to rest, unable to get comfortable, unable to tell
how much time was passing.

She settles slowly to the bottom of the water. She
looks up at swimmers. They are silent, just a few feet
above, splashing without sound. She sees only the parts
of their bodies that penetrate the water. Everything
else is foam and sunglow. She lies on her back at the

bottom of the surf, in the soft sand. She digs her fingers in. An inch or two below the surface, the sand is cooler. Everything floats on her eyes. Her eyes are the ocean. The ocean is her prayer. She can hold her breath forever.

"I got two of you asleep on me?" The Indian nurse clapped her hands.

The teenager was unconscious on the next cot. She wore only a black teeshirt with press-on letters spelling WENDY.

"I'm not asleep." Marian sat up. "I'm leaving."

Somebody had dumped her boots, skirt, books and handbag at the foot of the cot. The presence of her possessions seemed to have something to do with the return of feeling to her fingers.

"Okey-dokey." The nurse walked out.

Marian's watch fell out of her boot. Wendy's eyes snapped open.

"Hey, what's your favorite movie?" Wendy said.

"La Strada," Marian said. She loved the clown, Richard Basehart.

"La . . . what?"

"With Anthony Quinn. Da, da-da-dee-da . . ." Marian hummed the cornet theme.

"Oh yeah, I seen that one. I seen everything. Ask me. I love movies." Wendy lit a cigarette. "The only ones I don't like are those science-fiction ones. You know, weird guys in silver suits. Michael Rennie, stuff like that. You want to know why?"

Marian could not help thinking hard about this, and it made her feel faint again.

"It's because when the Martians, you know, turn up, they're always so perfect. I just wish they'd let them make mistakes, the way we do, instead of being perfect and then getting blown up in the end. It gives me the creeps the way they're always so perfect, those Martians."

"Me too." Marian made an oo*wee*oo science fiction sound.

"Yeah," Wendy said. "Oo*wee*oo is right."

"What's your name?" Marian said.

Wendy pinched her nipples and pulled the teeshirt forward. "What you see is what you get."

"That's an interesting name. I used to know somebody named Wendy."

"You knew somebody named Wendy? There must be two of me. Everybody thinks I'm somebody else. Does that ever happen to you?"

"No. I don't think so."

"Oo*wee*oo," Wendy said. "Weird."

"Well, yes," Marian said. "Maybe sometimes."

The receptionist ignored Marian's request for a receipt. She typed with one hand and waved her away with the other. She pointed to the chair where Marian had been sitting before the procedure. Jack had left a cone of flowers. His note said something about having to fill in at a baptism. She half-believed him, that was the awful thing.

She left the flowers.

She stood at the corner for twenty minutes waiting for a cab until she remembered that the two half-dollars, now ridiculously at room temperature, were all she had.

She stared into the window of the Woolworth's

across the street. Something unusual seemed to happen to the traffic when she crossed, bus doors wheezing
repeatedly. The store was in the middle of being remod-
eled. The whine of a circular saw sliced in and out of
the Muzak: a soft polka with imitation dog barks.

Convent life had bred in her the habit of celebrating
by herself: seeds would be the easiest thing to steal. She
hesitated next to the African violet potting soil. She
could slip the seeds in her handbag and she could say,
if challenged, that she had forgotten about them. She
spun the display rack and studied the vegetables. No,
she wanted flowers. Flowers would do nicely. Marigolds, here we are. She would sprout a white one and
win the Burpee's contest and go back to California tri-
umphant with twenty thousand dollars. But that
would take a couple of years. More maybe. It was worth
a try. She dropped the packet into her purse along with
some nasturtiums for good luck. Well, as Jack said
about Brooklyn, nasturtiums were somebody's idea of
beautiful. The National Flower of Brooklyn. The
Brooklyn Bridge was the National Flower of Brooklyn.
The bridge was beautiful, no question about it. Flowers.
Where the fuck was Jack?

She passed the sneakers, the dolls and the shoes. At
the candy counter she stopped, the smells clutching
her. Her mother used to be crazy about candy. Marian
scooped up some candy kisses and flipped them into her
mouth. The leftovers she dumped on the floor. White
furry monkeys bobbed on elastic strings. A little boy
with a patch over his eye tugged one and it spun franti-
cally, button eyes reflecting everything in the store.
She fondled a small spiral notebook. This was her plan:
she would take it to the checkout counter, have it
wrapped and then pretend to discover she'd left her

money home. Maybe she'd claim someone had picked
her purse. She giggled. Everybody stole from everybody else, that was the mortal necessity of it.

The checkout girls, small under their hair, were talking trousseaus.

"So when you getting married, Cecile?"

"June, I think." Neither of the girls acknowledged
Marian's stolen goods.

"I'm going to Denver for Carol's wedding."

"Whenzat?"

"June too."

"You better come to mine."

"When you getting married?"

"June. June, stupid."

"Oh yeah? You pregnant?"

"No, I'm not pregnant. I can get married anytime I
want. It's up to Vinnie. He says June. You better come,
Andrea, that's all I gotta say."

"Next please. Miss?"

Marian lowered her head and made for the door.

"Wait a minute, miss."

It was a man's voice. She kept going.

"Hey, hold it. You, miss."

Marian could see the checkout girls in the corner of
her eye, mouths half-open, gum visible, momentarily
unchomped.

The man was short, with a shiny face. His tie drooped
below his belt.

"Hold it, hold it, hold it. Come over here. Over here.
This way. No, this way, miss. I'm calling the cops. I saw
you. Cecile, Andrea, turn around. I'm calling the cops,
miss."

The manager's head pigeoned as he steered Marian
across the floor, past the carpenter, who took the nails

out of his mouth, and through the milky glass partition.

"Let's see that purse."

Marian collapsed in the swivel chair. The manager stuck his hand in her purse. Another polka, arf-arf, cheated through the door.

"I didn't say you could sit down or anything, miss. I'm calling the cops."

He dumped the contents of her purse on the floor. He spread out her rosary and the two seed packets and kicked some candy kisses out of the way. He straightened up and tucked his shirt in. He put his hands on his stomach.

"This is a very ticklish situation, young lady. I'm sick and tired of you people. Very ticklish."

"I'm sorry. I don't feel well."

"Yeah, sure. You people got a lot on your minds, I'm sure. I ought to call the cops."

His fingers were cold and slippery on her nipples. She put her hand on his, but did not lift it away. He unbuttoned the top of her blouse and put his hand in from above. "Very ticklish," he said.

Marian shoved him back. He sniffled and shook his head.

"Oh yeah? Well, I'm calling the cops. You want me to call the cops? I'm calling the cops, I swear to God. I'm sick of you people."

Marian turned around and took off her blouse. She spun the chair, covered her breasts and looked at him.

"You want the seeds?" he said. "I'll let you take the seeds."

Marian saw black spots, the ones the Indian nurse had asked her about. She shut her eyes slowly. The spots turned white: frail shadows of precious stones. She opened her eyes. Now they were red.

"I didn't do anything," she said.

"Keep the seeds. I said you can keep the seeds."

"It was all in my head. I wasn't even pregnant. The nervous system, that's the worst system in the whole body. I made it all up."

The manager weighed her breasts. "Nice," he said.

"From what he could see," Marian said, "I wasn't even pregnant."

She pressed the back of his neck, moist hairs swamping her fingers, and pulled him toward her. He resisted, looking up. She forced his face between her breasts. His breath was hot.

"Uruguay," she said. "Uruguay."

She kissed the manager on the lips, then covered herself and walked out. The trouble with Jack, like all the grand Jesuses of his generation, was that he still thought sinners wanted to be saved.

Eight

Father Sullivan gnawed his wrists like a puppy. He punched his knee ten times, felt nothing. He went from mirror to mirror, tracking the scent of himself. This room, his home, had forgotten him, as missionaries must be forgotten.

In his lap he held the chain from the dumbwaiter. The links were rectangular. He cleaned them with his handkerchief before slipping the chain around his neck. It couldn't be this banal. Where was the enormity of it?

Death by fire, death by drowning, death by falling, death by gunfire, death by sudden blows . . .

Cool fatherly death as Tolstoy taught it, warm motherly death the way the Irish loved it, death by pratfall, design or pride, stylish suicide with brandy and a revolver . . .

Sullivan, indoctrinated with heroism and stumblebum idealism, could imagine all of them vividly, movieize each death in his nerves. Not till now, though, had he felt the true tug of suicide. Catholics, just like everybody else, spent most of their time in despair, but what could be more distasteful than a dead priest?

The chain clanked on the pipe; he tried to silence it.

Once, when he was seventeen, in the surf off Rockaway, he'd hooked a bluefish out of a frenzied feeding school. It was a twelve-pounder, a holy fighter that ran him up and down the beach, ferociously fast, vengeful, like the Fish alive now in his stomach, his chest, his thighs, his throat: voracious, claiming—at last—the fisherman's life for his forage. He'd never felt so wanted.

He'd woken up in the shower with the Fish at his feet.

The Fish knew what to do. It knew exactly. It knew where to find the dumbwaiter outside his room in the rectory, it knew that the dumbwaiter chain would fit neatly around his neck, would slip right over the sprinkler pipe, would not require elaborate knotting, would do the job without mangling him. The Fish knew the chain would block his air supply the instant he stepped off the chair, would snap his neck, swallow his life, end him and be dead itself, satisfied, all extinguished. The Fish thought of everything.

Sullivan put a finger on his throat. His flesh was no longer his. It belonged to the links of chain, eagerly. He wiped them again. Washed his hands.

Covered his eyes like a child at a scary movie.

Went to the phone, keeping his eyes on the links rattling over his shoulders, slapping his stomach.

If she picked up on the first ring, he wouldn't do it.

"Natalie," he said.

"Yes. Hi."

"Natalie."

"What?"

"I'm going to kill myself."

"Why don't you come over here instead?"

"Okay. That's a good idea."

"What are you going to do right now, Jack?"

"Come over to your house."

"Right. And are you leaving right now?"

"Yeah. I'll see you in about forty minutes."

"I'll call you if you're not here in an hour."

"Thanks. That's a good idea."

"What do you mean, thanks? Are you thinking of not coming or something?"

"No. I'm okay. I'm on my way."

"Right now, Jack."

"Okay."

He picked up his souvenir Dodger baseball, autographed by the last team in Brooklyn's twilight. Looked at with its stitches a certain way, it seemed to smile. A baseball had the perfect heft for something you could throw forever. It was priceless. *Senza brama sicura richezza;* it was Dante's baseball. Natalie could catch it.

"Pete."

His father's name, he called it out loud.

"Pete."

But his father had no solution; he was in heaven, satisfied with small successes.

"Pete, please. Not now."

One thing his father would do: he implored the angels of his son's enemies not to wake the rest of hell. They agreed and flapped away, themselves relieved.

Sullivan toasted Pete's angel with a quick one for the road. He managed not to look down the dumbwaiter shaft on his way out.

There was a drunken Chinaman on crutches at the top of the stairs. On the Sea Beach Express another Chinaman offered him his seat, but Sullivan, spooked by the sinister dumbness of it, remained standing, exhausted by the glare that belonged to this time, this train and no other: part fluorescent dazzle, part honesty.

"How do you feel?" Through her silk blouse, Natalie's breasts told fascinating lies about the laws of gravity, perspective and light.

"I'm okay."

Sullivan walked into the living room, anxious to get as far as possible from the door. "I'm okay. This is life, I guess, and I'm still living it. How's Freddy?"

Natalie flipped a new braid over her shoulder. " 'I don't want to be a wife,' I say. And he says, 'I don't want to make you unhappy.' Stalemate. Something to do with chess, I guess. Freddy's in Houston buying himself something."

She went to the kitchen.

Sullivan lowered himself cautiously onto the couch. He monitored the fly that was cruising alone in the middle of the room. The television was tuned to a talking head, sound off. The record player was on. Sullivan watched the tone arm breathe on a warped disk: "Both Sides Now," Joni Mitchell. That slut. She tried to pick him up once at a Mobilization rally on Central Park West. She autographed his cast, adding her phone number in lipstick. He was perhaps the only Catholic in the world aware that Joni Mitchell had copped the idea for "Both Sides Now" from a line in *Henderson the Rain King.* Interesting. His first smile since suicide.

"Turn it off," Natalie said. "And the TV too. TV's a lousy lay."

The fly plinked against the window and then, as if someone had called its name, flew straight for the open door.

He recognized the faded red hammock from Jaipur.

"One needs a new sofa," Natalie shouted. She had been unable to arrange her apartment in a way that made conversation possible.

Sullivan was curious about the fire escape. The window was painted shut. Prisoners saw windows in a special way. He punched it twice and managed to raise it high enough so that in a crouch he was able to stick his head outside. The stars twitched like confetti on water.

"How is it out there?"

"Cool and gorgeous." He tucked his head inside and sneezed.

"Cool and gorgeous like me, huh?"

"Right." He punched the window shut. He followed her laugh into the kitchen. She'd taken off her jeans and draped them over the refrigerator door while she groped for a can of Metrecal and smoothed her panties, ripe pink in the glow of the appliance bulb. Her lips were poised in the attack position for the letter G.

"I killed someone," Sullivan said.

Natalie folded her jeans, tucked them neatly in the freezer compartment and shut the door. She sipped the Metrecal and regarded him moistly.

"How like me," she said. "I always go soft for exotic men."

She was flattering someone, herself or him, Sullivan couldn't be sure.

"You smell like a brewery," she said, suddenly bub-
bling over like a child organizing a game. "Let's take
a shower. I'll get some towels. I'll be with you in a
minute. I just have to call the weather bureau first."
"Now?"
"It's supposed to snow again, do you believe it?
Maybe they'll cancel classes tomorrow." The icebox
whinnied, then was quiet.
"Are you kidding?" Sullivan was still a little serious
from suicide.
"The bathroom's right over there."
Natalie aimed him across the room, lifting off his
sweater on the way, squeezing his neck and depositing
him at the bathroom door. She went back to the phone.
Sullivan thought he saw her lips move twice before she
hung up and went to the bedroom.
The receiver clucked when he picked it up. It was
warm from the heat of her hand and ear. There was no
honor among flirts.
The bathroom featured a white ceramic toilet-paper
holder in the shape of cupped hands. Everything else
was black, except the shower curtain, still dripping
from recent use, the droplets irrigating a white swan,
a woman (Oriental again!) with a kerchief, otherwise
naked, a boat with several sails, a scaly fish and red
butterflies in a storm. Another silk blouse was strewn
along the shower rod, soft, despondent, a cut flower
recalling its native field.
Death by drowning. . . .
Sullivan turned the shower on very hot and found a
toothbrush with warped bristles. He glanced continu-
ously in the mirror, which soon was ghosted with
steam.
Toothpaste fringed his beard. Without consulting

himself, he'd decided to shave. The only razor he could find was pearl-handled, evidently Natalie's. His beard was piebald, more gray on the left. As it disappeared, he was surprised to discover that his mouth was set in a tireless smile. And yes, there was one pale cheekbone on the right, another on the left. Everything symmetrical as an icon, except for the hive under his left eye, slightly off-center, a momentary blemish. This could be the last time he saw himself alive. He saluted himself as a stranger. Nothing touch.

He dumped his clothes in a pile, counting the pieces twice, each time with a different result.

Natalie's blouse fluttered into the tub and got soaked before he could grab it. He turned his soft new face to the spray and adjusted the nozzle just short of stinging.

He heard the door open, waited for Natalie to say something. The door closed, not a word. He parted the shower curtain. Natalie had taken his clothes and hung a blue terrycloth robe on the knob. He let the shower run. He doused his face, rubbed the hair on his belly in a circular pattern. He laughed, stopped, reminded himself that he owed her a certain amount of sincerity; gentlemen were not supposed to smile at this point. His conscience, in its own way, was scrupulous, topiary.

Where *was* he? Rajasthan. Where was Marian?

She was not a mother, he was not a father.

Natalie had her jeans back on. She lay diagonally across the brass four-poster and she was looking something up in *TV Guide*. Sullivan turned up the radio, then turned it off.

"Well, you look a hundred percent better," she said.

"I feel better, thanks. How come you put your jeans in the icebox?'"

"It feels terrific when I put them back on."

She tugged playfully at his hip. "How come you say 'icebox' instead of 'refrigerator'?"

"Only Jesuits say 'refrigerator.'"

"Jesuits, Jesuits, Jesuits! What is it with those guys anyway? They just won't go away, will they; they're worse than the fucking Beatles."

She smiled, the corners of her mouth turned in sharply, tasting something. "How's the leg?"

"Pretty good. Stiff once in a while, that's all."

She sighed and let the *TV Guide* flop to the floor. "That's the trouble with you foreign missionaries. You're interesting, but once you break down, it's impossible to get parts for you."

"It's lucky we weren't all killed," Sullivan said.

"The car crash was the least of it, let's face it." She rolled over. "And since when has a little death ever stopped you? You're a Catholic, aren't you?"

Sullivan stroked the inverted valentine of her rump. "Don't touch me while I'm being fat."

She got up and turned the overhead light off. Sullivan felt the walls recede. He took off his robe and waited for her under the covers. She undressed quietly at the foot of the bed, her body haloed briefly by the beam of a passing bus. Seeing her naked for the first time dismissed all his dreams. She lay down on her belly, cozily ignoring him, a faint creamy shine on the left cheek of her ass, which was full but rather flat. A cliplight silhouetted her shoulders against the *khadi* painting of Krishna and the Gopis, something Freddy had salvaged from India, a memento of the love they'd earned.

"The only thing is," she said, "I have a headache."

"Would you like some water?"

"And an aspirin, please."

The bathroom was still fogged up. He pried open the aspirin tin, dropped the contents into the pocket of his robe, filled a glass at the sink, turned off the light with a nod of his chin against the wall switch, which made a sound like a cockroach being crushed, and step by step, savoring the balance between desire and the fear of capture, while water coughed in the pipes, he made his way back to her bed in the ribboned dark.

She was huddled, her back to him. She rolled over, blinked at the glass, aimed it at her lips, swallowed audibly.

"Bless you, Father." She massaged his eyelids, her fingertips still cool from the glass.

They began to sweat. Her smell was mushrooms and peaches. They explored for things too close to see. She moistened her fingers and began masturbating him. He slid his hand up her leg; she resisted only enough to let him feel how strong her thighs were: yet smooth, feathery almost. She groaned, a bit of eyeshine and naked sincerity as she rolled her head. She turned on her stomach and reached for the sides of the mattress, pressing her body down, spreading her thighs. He took two steps on his knees and dipped his cock between her legs. He was hard as a tree.

"The cream," she said.

"Where?"

The jar was just out of reach. He stretched, dropped the cap, hesitated, decided how to proceed, took a deep breath, swabbed his cock with the cream and smeared some between her buttocks. He grunted away from the night table and lowered himself on her.

He stopped on the first thrust. Everything stopped.
She was the first to cry out. It was as if they'd inhaled
at the same time and found no air to breathe.

"What is it?" Natalie flopped on her back. "What is
it? What is it?"

There was lightning in his prick.

"Oh my God," she said.

He grabbed the jar.

Vicks VapoRub.

Natalie disappeared behind the shower curtain uttering small "ohs" with every step. Sullivan scrambled
in right behind her. "Oh." They bumped together,
"oh," he nearly lost his balance, "oh." Natalie lathered
furiously. "There's not much hot water," she said.
"Hurry up. Oh."

Somewhere in the spray and the steam and slippery
blind stinging, he came upon a bar of soap. He scrubbed
her, she scrubbed him. They shrieked, laughed. The
shower curtain butterflies shimmied. He jumped out of
the tub and grabbed a towel and buffed himself dry,
rubbing his crotch as hard as he could to induce a
competing, more manageable pain. His stomach and
his prick and his thighs were inflamed and he wondered if this was a serious injury and suddenly he
missed the sound of her laughter and he knew this was
bad and he forgot to breathe.

The gunshot echoed off the black tiles like an exploding scream. Sullivan threw his arms over his head and
stood in a half-crouch. Smoke bit into his nostrils. Plaster flaked on his hair.

"There's a phone call for you, Father."

Freddy stood stiffly in the doorway, as if wearing

spurs. His eyes jingled. The Magnum was leveled at Sullivan's balls. He felt very cold.

"You can walk!" Sullivan couldn't breathe.

"Not exactly." Freddy tapped the gun barrel on the crutch beside him. "But I can fly."

He twisted toward Natalie, who was wrapped in the shower curtain, standing slowly out of a squat.

"I bought a two-engine Mitsubishi, Natch. Five passengers. Cruises at four-fifty. Seven hours from Houston, including a stop at Columbus."

Sullivan hoped Freddy wasn't going to run out of things to say about his new plane. He exhaled.

Natalie stepped out of the tub and turned her back to them. "Why don't you get the phone, Jack?"

"The phone?" He couldn't understand what she wanted.

"It's Moose," Freddy said. "Take it in the living room."

"Hello, Monsignor." Water from Sullivan's legs puddled by Freddy's desk. Natalie listened in an ice-trance of anger.

"How are you, Jack?" Monsignor MacMurray said. Sullivan could hear the Knicks game in the background. Overtime. "You must be bushed, Jack. That's some mess you made out of the dumbwaiter. It's going to cost an arm and a leg to fix it."

"Sorry, Moose."

"Don't tell me you're sorry. Sorry is boring. And forget about that clown of a nun. The church needs smart guys like you. I want you to throw yourself into your work."

"Where's Marian?"

"Lay off the nuns, Jack. Nuns are too tight a fit."

"Where's Marian?"

"She's okay."

"Where is she, Moose?"

"She's cooling her heels in the convent, I guess. What am I running, a dating service?"

"Sorry."

"Yeah. Watch out, Jack. Jealousy is a harder thing than anybody's dick. Listen, is that Powers guy still there? His wife's been trying to get a hold of me, and when I called back, he answered. Put him on."

Sullivan handed the phone to Freddy and slumped against the hammock. Natalie opened a window. The breeze carried the smell of Vicks from her.

Monsignor MacMurray's voice, pint-sized and piercing, strutted from the receiver: "Powers, hello. This is Monsignor MacMurray again. Listen, Powers, was that a gun I heard go off?"

"No, Monsignor."

"Don't lie to me, Powers. I'm not as dumb as I look."

"Sorry, Monsignor."

"Forget it. You're understandably upset. Listen, Powers, you're a wealthy guy, right?"

"Well . . ."

"Well, I want you to recollect what Our Lord had to say about wealthy guys and heaven and camels and the eye of a needle. You're passing through the eye of that needle right now. Here's what I want you to do: first I want you to get down on your knees."

"I can't, Monsignor. I'm a cripple."

"Aren't we all, Powers? Aren't we all? Just bow your head, in that case, and make the Act of Contrition."

"Me? What for, Monsignor? What'd I do?"

"For one thing, Powers, you probably got so much dough you're guilty before you even get up in the morning. And for lying to me about the gun. That's the second and seventh commandments right there, not to mention a probable intention to break the fifth: *Thou shalt not kill*, Powers."

"Tell that to his Eminence," Natalie said softly.

"Now look, Powers, get a move on. Do you want absolution or don't you?"

"Over the phone, Monsignor?"

"Why not?"

Freddy was crying by the time he finished his Act of Contrition.

"C'est folie pûre," Natalie said. "I guess I'm just too unhappy to have a good affair."

"Okay, Powers, that's enough. Now for your penance, I want you to get a job. Learn a trade. *Do* something. Throw yourself into your work. And listen, do me a favor and tell Father Sullivan I've assigned him to six-thirty Mass this week and I expect him in my office immediately afterwards. Good night, now. All of you get some rest. And, Powers . . ."

"Yes, Monsignor?" Freddy pivoted like a child.

"Try spending some time with the little lady once in a while, why dontcha?"

They found Duke Farrell where he fell, half a block from home. His tiny red transistor radio was still tuned to the stock-market report, the *News* was still in his hand, most of the *Bay Ridge Spectator* had blown away. Peanuts' mother had gone shopping and Duke had taken a walk to get the papers, and when he turned into the wind from the bay, it stopped his heart.

Where is God? God is everywhere.

Peanuts dreamed he was with his grandfather when he died. He saw him swaggering down the street the way he used to. He began to sing and fall down at the same time. It was a beautiful song; Peanuts knew it without having heard it before. He held his grandfather in his arms and he felt the final thumps of his heart. He was happy to be with him. Nobody stutters when they sing.

Peanuts woke with a start and didn't know where he was.

Where is God? God is everywhere.

Duke's cronies let Peanuts tend bar at the wake. They approved of the way he always poured such a generous shot. They came in suits and ties worn only at wakes. They drank and they drank and they exchanged jokes about their departed friend, whose blue burial suit was sagging right along with the rest of them. The women took refuge in statistics: age, amount of insurance, the hour of death, the instant of the dark angel's arrival—everything was covered—the bright soul's ascension, the arrows of grace, everything.

"Put a head on this, will you, kid. Thanks. How many times I seen yer grandfather run out from under his hat going after a long fly, I can't begin to tell you, Dennis. . . ."

"Turn his back to the plate, he would, and take off like a bat out of hell. . . ."

"A great arm he had as a young man. . . ."

"A dangerous arm. Gimme a refill, Dennis. Attaboy."

Green Gaffney was the only one not wearing a blue suit. He had on, as always, his World War I cavalryman's uniform, complete with ceremonial sword. He never took it off. He was prone to blinking.

"I hope you don't mind my saying this, Jim," Green Gaffney confided to Peanuts' father, "but the Duke doesn't look all that bad, now does he? You'd hardly know he was sick. Looks like he's even got a bit of a tan. You got to hand it to the Maguires. They do a terrific job, don't they? It's an art it itself, painting a stiff."

Peanuts waited to hear something about his grandfather's batting ability, but this never seemed to come up. He washed four dozen highball glasses. The brogues of the wrinkled old men mixed with the rusty whispers of the women; everything sounded like the suck and gargle of the sink.

The second day of the wake, he excused himself with a bow that drew admiring chuckles. On his way to the subway he passed Fogarty's house, the only brick house on the block, the house his grandfather had fallen in front of. Peanuts expected the sidewalk to be stained. It wasn't. A red snow shovel was propped against the fireplug. Jack Fogarty's kid brother was pressing his nose against the porch window. He jumped away and disappeared into the hollow shadows.

This was it, this was the place. Another twenty steps and Duke would have been in sight of his own house. Here's where he fell. The Fogarty kid must have seen it happen, been frightened and ducked away, just like now, without a word. Which was why the cops who found the body—no wallet, no ID—shipped the Duke straight to the morgue without family, slipping the DOA tag on his big toe. They inventoried his hat, his shoes, his flashlight.

———

Peanuts took the Fourth Avenue Local headed downtown. He sat across the aisle from a high school girl and looked up her skirt. She sniffed indignantly. Greek maybe, probably Italian.

Where is God? God is everywhere.

The girl joined her hands and crossed her shins, firm pacific swords.

Peanuts got out at Eighteenth Street and headed down toward the bay. The streets were nearly empty. Wind gusted the hat from an old man wearing alert new rubbers. Peanuts ran after it, sidestepping a bus. He ran with sublime anchorless speed. For the sake of a stranger's hat dancing down the street, he did not believe in death. He stopped a truck. He scooped up the hat. He handed it to the old man, who spit with embarrassment. Peanuts bounded away. Hatman to the rescue.

The Gowanus Canal smelled like a laundry and was a unique shade of green.

Peanuts stood under the elevated highway that vaulted out of Red Hook and cast its humming shadow on the canal. The sun was bright and dry and the wind just cold enough to make him keep his hands in his pockets. Along the embankment, torn sheets of industrial plastic flapped in the ailanthus trees, knobbly where the leaves had left them. Peanuts looked back toward Bay Ridge and the church spires on the hills, the houses lined up below, snug and devout. Behind him a squad car prowled.

He started down the embankment, the slope not

steep enough to make him skid. He skipped over a twisted stack of venetian blinds and fluorescent light fixtures, things that got tossed away not because they didn't work but because they'd lived their lives. The embankment got steeper; he took his hands out of his pockets. Cans crunkled underfoot. He clambered around a pile of smashed pallets and broken wine bottles, praying no glass would pierce his sneakers.

He stood finally at the edge of the canal. It was glassy but without reflections. He clenched his teeth and breathed through his mouth. He unbuttoned his fly, and with a deep spinal satisfaction, he peed in the canal, and the whole world, just like him, was speechless.

Where is God? God is everywhere.

Nine

Evenings Father Sullivan drank. Chocolate-chip cookies washed down with Cutty. Mornings he moped through his Mass with the dreamlike feeling of trudging around in one shoe.

Another week or so and that would be the end of it, the Latin Mass: the astounding non sequiturs, the glowing sacrifice fringed with et ceteras. He was going to miss it. It was the narrative model for his life. The new Vulgate Mass was well-intentioned, but a little too Las Vegas Lutheran for his taste. Loyola's *Exercises,* of course, were the truest, most rabbinical Mass. Then there was Stendhal. But he hadn't read a really good Mass since *Under the Volcano.*

Could Marian have cut her hair? Had she put on weight? Would her chin wrinkle when she smiled? Could she smile? These questions shadowed him all during his six-thirty Mass.

In the first pew he spotted a woman who looked like Marian. By the Last Gospel, however, she was snoring. She did not even stir when the Kennedy kid tripped, dumping the missal. Still, there was merit in the clumsiest worship, the truth's final disguise.

On a hunch he spent Monday afternoon in the coffee shop across from Sister Carmela's brownstone on Henry Street. There were three skinny waitresses and a wino curious about his cassock. French fries to the left of him, cherry pie drooling on his right. He stared at his bacon, sugared his thumb on a glazed doughnut, sucked it. He saw Marian coming out of the subway. She *had* done something to her hair. No.

Wait. It *was* Marian. Her hair was the same, but she'd taken to wearing sunglasses propped on the roof of her head. She crossed the street like a city kid; she strolled like a woman with a new appreciation of music. He tried to concentrate through the whimperings of Liszt and the stink of hamburger grease. She was a newsreel: look at her clothes, look at her shyness, imagine her words in the furry ear of the sightless newsdealer.

Just before she disappeared, she tucked her sunglasses into the second button of her blouse, exposing a bit of freckled cleavage. She looked cheerful and well-aimed. Was she breakfasting with strangers?

The cheeseburger he ordered medium-rare arrived exactly that way. Sullivan shifted on his stool and sipped his tea like a spy.

The next morning Marian walked Sister Carmela's dog, that dumb Dalmatian. A high percentage of the breed was born deaf, but how they loved to chase cars! Impatiently he ordered more tea.

———

Wednesday he bought a '58 Chrysler Windsor, a perfect crewcut of a car. He had neglected, however, to
renew his driver's license. He bought a hammock for
his room and tried writing in it, but this made him feel
like a kid shivering in a backyard tent. He bought a
copy of *Rubber Soul* and gave himself a wicked paper
cut on the record sleeve, so he tuned to an ethnic station that played circusy music. He spent six bucks on
a rare *Aquaman* comic, tossing it away when he came
to a balloon that said: "Oh frogmen with your slippery
flippers save me! I hear the bubbles of saboteurs escaping underwater!" The light was pale, passionless, always the light of an alleyway.

He came to his senses Thursday morning at the desk
of a midtown hotel he couldn't remember checking in
to. His new belt, with a rodeo buckle, was missing some
loops in his pants. He was wearing a blazer that identified him as a member of a tuna-fishing tournament.
The badge said Captain. He wondered who he'd traded
his cassock to this time. He paid for his room with
singles.

He made breakfast once, broke a glass, was startled
by the smell of toast. Clumsy cops moved furniture in
his head. He masturbated twice Friday evening, his
semen splattering on the linoleum in an appealing
shape, something like a half-dreamed map of Spain. He
enumerated his One True Faiths: the Cubs, Lionel
trains, dry-fly fishing, legendary unclimbable peaks

whose glaciers wept fear, Johnny Carson's monologue, and things you couldn't do anything about: wind, slow sex, sun, the will of a strong woman. Whenever he stuck his hands in his pockets, cellophane crackled. This was glass raining.

Next week he went on the wagon. He just did it. He immediately detected a change in his blood pressure. His skin bristled, his blood bubbled. Exhilarating but unbearable, the intense delicacy of the addict denying himself. By ten in the morning he was deeply in love with Bev, the waitress. She had done something to her foot requiring her to walk on her heel, rear end jutting out, torso swiveling, a wounded walk. She seemed, like him, to be more alive than her job allowed.
"Can I get a corn muffin to go?"
"Definitely."
Her hands reminded him of Marian's.

That evening, rather than continue in the hell of the temporarily saved, he started drinking again. He tied on an unpleasant, rational drunk with six straight whiskeys, then lost count. He passed out, woke up dehydrated, still dreaming. He saw a burning building where Marian kissed him good-bye with her eyes open. He felt certain she was beside him, but it was only a body memory, like the outline of a piece of furniture against the wall after it'd been moved. Her absence was changing from the terrible uncontrolled pain of tearing away to this misperception of shadows—this momentary, infrequent forgetting that she just wasn't there anymore. Her smoky hair, the shine of her shins, the soft muscles they discovered together, the fathomless rippling of her cunt—he couldn't summon them up, not even the smell of her, not her face, nor the freckles on her insteps.

He slept, woke, drank, went to the corner for cigarettes. He kept swallowing.

Friday he didn't see her either. Saturday he found himself at the door of Sister Carmela's brownstone. The lighted bell over her mail slot went ding-dong.

"I think it was the snow," Marian said, "that made me love you. Hold on, there's someone on the phone."

He waited, feeling he was about to fall backward. Finally, frantic for whiskey, he ran down the stoop before she returned. He didn't see her again till he followed her to the Be-In.

A tall girl lay on her side, naked to the waist in the tirelessly dancing tips of grass. The sun, threading its way through several aromas, lit her hips. Everyone's hairstyle looked contrived.

Sister Marian was carrying four pink balloons. Her mint sundress bloomed in the breeze. She couldn't have been a better beacon, but Father Sullivan was worried he'd lose her.

"Need a hand carrying those?"

She flinched. An unfamiliar crease appeared, then vanished at the corner of her mouth.

"I can handle them, thanks." She shifted her newspaper to the hand carrying the balloons.

"Where are you headed?"

"Just wandering."

Aged. She'd aged on her own.

"Lots of people here," he said.

"A little too close together for their own good, I'd say." The crease reappeared, a wrinkle.

"Like trees." He was still a couple of steps behind her. He strummed his stubble.

"Exactly." She spoke firmly and politely, as if entertaining a visitor. "But if we were talking about trees, I'd say thin them out." She swapped the balloons and the Sunday *Times* again. "When trees are thinned, they grow more amply, are healthier and provide just as much shade. You've seen one-sided trees, haven't you? Also, during storms, trees too close together clash limbs, causing injury and damage."

"What kind of trees are those?"

"Tall and skinny."

"I see. Where are you going?"

"I like to watch trees at night, only you can't really see them."

"Only in the movies. Can I give you a lift?"

"I have to get back to work soon."

"Work? On Sunday? Where?"

"Sunday's a big day for *you,* isn't it? I work at the Botanical Gardens. I give lectures to school outings and I work in the greenhouse. Weekends are busy."

A black man, his eyes tobaccoey yellow, was playing a washboard with thimbles. Next to him a young woman in a jumpsuit blew an amplified harmonica.

"I have a car," Sullivan said.

"You can find music everywhere these days," Marian said.

A little girl tugged her arm. "Bloon, bloon, bloon!" she yelled. Marian gave her one.

"Go be nice to someone else," Sullivan said. "They'll give you another balloon."

"Where?" the little girl asked.

A single-engine plane, yellow with white stripes—a stiff canary—popped through the sky's lone cloud, soaring, buzzing, droning.

The bay waters of the Narrows were braided by a mild breeze, the sky was simple blue. There were no leaves on the trees yet, only outlines of buds, pale green and pink.

Sullivan parked his Chrysler on Shore Road and they walked along the bicycle path holding hands, swinging arms. At Bay Ridge Avenue, by the old ferry slip, a woman who might have been Mrs. Garrity hollered yoo-hoo after a bus. Tonight at the rectory she would nag Sullivan about the bus leaving her behind, about how nobody in the world had no consideration anymore and how sick and tired she was getting of TV.

They approached a thick grove of birches, waiting, the way birches always were, to be peeled.

Marian held the paper at arm's length, challenging the society pages.

"Announcement has been made," she began, "by Mr. and Mrs. Elkins Wetherill of Plymouth Meeting, Pa., and Waldboro, Maine, of the engagement of their daughter, Alexandra Wetherill, blahblahblah . . . the prospective bride, an alumna—oh, I love the *Times*'s Latin . . ."

"Fucking Protestants," Sullivan said. "They think pleasure is the coward's way out."

". . . an alumna of the Springside School, Bennett Junior College and the University of Pennsylvania class of '63, attends Pennsylvania's School of Veterinary Medicine, blahblahblah . . . her father is a partner in Brown Brothers Harriman and chairman of the executive committee of the Union Pacific Corporation . . ."

The shade flickered on her words. Sullivan's eyes were at grass level, watching new-hatched gnats wobble. He punched the newspaper.

"You want to get married?" he asked.

She spit in his face. The sensation was deafening.

He managed to light a cigarette. "Is that a definite no, then?"

"Nosiree. I mean, yes. Yes. Only, from now on, watch it, okay?"

His cigarette was soggy. He dropped it, the fossil of an awful future.

Somewhere, across the baseball diamonds separating the bay and the apartment houses, an old plastic radio was playing, plugged into an inflammably installed extension cord that snaked through the dandelions. And somewhere, along one of the third-base lines, sweat was steaming up from the grizzled chest hairs of a Transit Authority retiree, blending with strands of barbecue smoke that floated, twitching occasionally, over the windless outfields where a city-bred kitten, unfamiliar with spring and grass and open space, stumbled. Kids played, people dozed. The sun pinked them. Parents taught first words.

Father Sullivan and Sister Marian were deeper in the birches. His hands were folded. She put hers on them. He kissed her fingers, tilting forward. She withdrew her hands with a sigh of disapproval and meshed his fingers one by one, mockingly, as if to say: I could make a sweater out of you, then unravel the whole thing if I wanted.

She twisted his wrists and ran her nails across them. "Here, let me help you cut your wrists. You're not a family man."

The first time he'd seen her in the street, he'd imagined she was pregnant: something about the way she gathered her skirt when she ran to the old nun, kept clutching it as if the cloth itself were her heart. And when she told him that she was a nun, he'd felt at once that she, not Sister Raymond Marjorie, was the injured one, had been injured at birth and would always, despite her eagerness, bear a wound: that is, she was truly a nun. Now the same wet shock and tenderness was in her eyes, and again he couldn't get over the illusion that he'd tripped her in the eighth month of a pregnancy.

Her hair fell behind her like a cloud. He touched her cheek. Her chin. Her eyebrows. She closed her eyes. Her eyelids. He touched her chin.

"You know," he said, "there are people nobody touches from day to day, from year to year. . . ."

"What are you teasing me for?" She smiled at him, as at the arrival of a pet.

The second time he kissed her, her lips got slippery. He listened to her breathing become louder, taking her whole body with it. Sullivan touched her, blinder and blinder, a blind man, finally, who'd lost all patience and all sense of direction. His dream of dying fell from him like a stone.

Their passion was brief, intense, a battering uncontrollable seizure. He could hardly hold her and she was incapable of holding herself. When it was over they were both drenched. She was panting; her scalp was slippery with sweat. She fondled his penis, all her attention focused there, a serious child with a flower. His slow smile widened, hers danced off her face. Her foot slid across his stomach and down his hips. Flies found their sweat.

"Okay, Father. On your feet."

McSweeney's toothpick made all the difference. The journalist, the lethal shot-putter, the cop—he shifted his toothpick from one side of his tongue to the other.

Sullivan's insides shuddered to a stop. He was on his feet, he was forgetting Marian and he was looking at McSweeney, who just stood there silently, toothpick dangling, an antenna. He was a good ten years younger than Sullivan. He was thicker and tougher. Already his head looked as if it had ducked too often. He was a rough piece of work with a job that made him rougher, and he knew how, by waiting, to make his menace grow. His clothes were tired. He was a cop all right.

Marian pulled down her skirt. She crushed leaves. "C'mere, Father."

Sullivan hesitated, looking over his shoulder. "What for?" He was trying to map where McSweeney's gun was. McSweeney yanked him closer and flipped open his wallet to display the badge.

"Over here, Father."

McSweeney still had the badge in his hand when they came to a stop. He held it there and looked back at Marian, who stood up. Sullivan froze, as if he'd grasped a cold pipe; if he bolted now, he'd tear his flesh away.

"You know, Father, this is a public place. I ought to take you both down to the station." He tweezered the toothpick between his thumb and pinkie and pointed through the birches. The flat end of the toothpick was shredded.

Sullivan saw the whip aerial shooting up from the rear fender of a black Dodge; he saw the outline of another man in the front seat. The outline included a uniform cap. He felt oddly reassured. McSweeney was behaving like a cop and a cop was not impossible to deal with. Sullivan might still know, somewhere, how to handle him.

"Do you have to do this?" Sullivan rattled some change in his pocket.

Marian seemed to be avoiding the light.

"Just wait here, Father." McSweeney took a step toward Marian.

Sullivan reached for his arm, but before he touched it, McSweeney turned. He was quick for a man his size.

"Look, Father. I'd like to have a little fun, too. Wait here."

Sullivan relaxed, then collected his muscles into a spring and bent his knees slightly, leaning toward McSweeney, not looking in his eyes but at his neck, at the spot he was going to lunge at and rip open. McSweeney tucked in his chin.

"Fine. Okay, Father. You want to come along to the station, then? Let's go. That'd be a pretty sight, wouldn't it. Pacifist priest and ex-nun booked for fucking al fresco."

"Everybody has their own war, McSweeney."

"Sure, Father. C'mon. Let's go."

"No."

"Whaddaya mean no? Your ass is grass, Father."

"Look, I mean no. The girl's a virgin. She's a virgin, McSweeney."

"You don't say? From the looks of her, I'd say she was knocked up." McSweeney ogled Marian, then shifted a step closer to Sullivan, smirking. "Say, you wouldn't happen to have any Polaroids or anything, would you?"

"What?"

"Forget it." He replaced the toothpick on his tongue. "I thought priests were supposed to tell the truth, Father. You better move that car of yours or I'll have to give you a ticket."

"Okay," Sullivan said, choking.

McSweeney started to walk away, turned.

"Oh Father?"

"Yeah?"

"I thought we'd be seeing you at the demonstration outside the UN today. There's something big supposed to happen."

"I'll be there."

"That's swell. See ya, Father."

Sullivan didn't budge till he saw the whip aerial twitch when McSweeney sat in the car. The cops—the silhouettes of McSweeney and his partner—talked to one another, looked around and shook their heads hilariously. Sullivan turned Marian the other way. He heard the car start and drive slowly off.

He stuffed his shirt in his pants: all the while he'd been facing McSweeney, his shirt flap had been sticking out of his fly.

Marian was pale. "Who was that? Don't I know that guy from somewhere?"

Sullivan told her they got a warning to move the car.

———

They bought hot dogs and Cokes on Third Avenue
and drove downtown. The silence, like something
stepped on and stuck to their shoes, would not move
away. The streets were dead except for the ghosts of
ancient cars, all claiming to be the spirit of Henry
Ford, quarreling about whose claim was the likeliest.

They headed for the East River Drive via the Brooklyn Bridge. Marian read aloud from a small book about
bonsai.

It was pleasant, like being temporarily blind, or
being tended to while required to see only a few things:
the roadbed humming, the occasional seagull, skid
marks. The bridge advanced with huge dragon strides
over the waterfront and the river, plunging with assurance into both mediums, making the land seem soft
and the water shallow. Expansion joints ticked under
their tires.

Sullivan was driving too fast. He wanted to get there.
Henry Ford didn't hate walking, but he sure spoiled it
for lots of people. *He wanted to get there.*

"I'd love to go to Japan," Marian said. "Wouldn't
you?"

He could still taste their passion under the birches as
something which might have been a fact, like an address he once lived at, or his weight.

They parked across from the General Assembly
building. The wind chanted. Eighty-three member flags
flapped, keeping time. Forty or so Catholic Workers
were marching on either side of the Powers' Land
Rover.

Natalie, in her red angora sweater, hopped on the
hood, where a spare tire was mounted, wartlike.

Roberta MacNamara, one of the oldest Catholic Workers, nearly eighty and still diligent, placed a saffron-colored cushion on the spare tire so Natalie could sit comfortably.

She pulled her feet over her thighs into the lotus position. She exchanged a few words with Alice. She bowed her head while someone else, a boy in a peacoat, splashed gasoline over her from a white plastic container.

When Natalie's sweater was saturated, the boy stepped back. Economically, as if beginning a story, she shook her braids over her shoulder.

Then, with an almost imperceptible motion, Natalie struck a match.

McSweeney took pictures.

Ten

Sister, I love your skin, I love your eyes, I love your folding arms, Sister, I love your fingers, I love your legs, I love you when you sit down, Sister, I want to lick your belly, I love your night, Sister, I love you when you turn away, you are my mother tongue, I hear you like a bell, Sister, I love you.

Peanuts woke at the bottom of his bed, crouched against his dream of Sister Marian making her way through a storm of cantaloupe seeds.

The sensation of seeds pelting him lingered on his skin like an urgent but indecipherable message while he shook his Cheerios out of the carton. Peanuts dreamed every night of Sister Marian. There'd been no official comment on her sudden disappearance from school, her place having been filled by Sister Monica, who was full of stories about where the snakes wound up on leaving Ireland: in Soviet Russia, East Germany, Harvard and North Korea, inciting anticlerical atrocities, mostly live burials, along the way.

More Cheerios. Peanuts detested them, but he

needed four more boxtops for a plastic Green Beret.

He bit the old Band-Aid off his thumb and put on a fresh one; he'd sliced himself climbing up from the Gowanus Canal. He decided to wear his altar boy outfit to church. It would be a terrible thing to get caught wearing the cassock and surplice on the street, but doing it seemed to answer his dream, so he ordered himself to feel invisible and brave. He tucked the switchblade in his belt.

He squinted at the dawn and jumped off the stoop and sprinted down the block, surplice flapping. He galloped under the rainbow fanning from Dr. McCarthy's garden sprinkler; he slapped the hood of the bucktoothed Roadmaster on the corner. The breeze from the bay rinsed the streets, a sigh of relief. It was great getting up early this time of the year.

Peanuts heard the wings before the words:

"I AM THE ONE, I AM THE ONE WHO DREAMS ALL NIGHT IN BRIGHT WHISPERS, I AM THE ONE WHO HEARS YOU MURMUR: GIVE ME MORE, GIVE ME LESS. I AM THE ANGEL OF THE EAST, I AM THE ONE WHO HEARS INDIANS WEEP. I AM ANGRY AND PROUD. I SPEAK ALL LANGUAGES BEAUTIFULLY. I AM THE ONE WHO LOVES THE THINGS OF CHILDREN. I LOVE COMIC BOOKS, PEZ DISPENSERS, DAMP SMELLS. I LOVE YOU. SPEAK . . ."

In the window of the luncheonette Peanuts caught sight of him, a black and bristling library of feathers, Uruguay, ready to pounce.

Then he saw it was only himself, rippling like a tropical fish in the crookedly installed window. He stepped to within arm's length of the window. His white surplice reflected clearly; the black of his cassock only darkened the Pepsi display on the shelves.

He leaned in close enough for his breath to mist the glass. Now I'm black and white, Uruguay, like Sister Marian. He studied the disembodied reflection of his face, especially his lips. Ovals of mist, miniature lungs, swelled and sagged on the glass as he whispered:

"I hear you like a bell, Sister, I love you."

The sunlight slanted across the church doors, liquefying the grapevines worked in wood, eddying through the tendrils, leaves and fruits. The light pooled, stilled. Someone had just unlocked the church doors.

Yes, at last he would speak. He would make a good confession. To Father Sullivan, a foreign missionary who'd soon be wandering off among the pagans, he'd tell his lust for Sister Marian, vividly, in detail, no sins of act or imagination left out. It wouldn't be so bad. It'd be fine, in fact, like confiding his crimes to an itinerant executioner who had no special interest in hanging him. If he could speak to a pane of glass in the street, he'd find a way to talk to Father Sullivan.

Monsignor MacMurray was standing in the sacristy, all vested up and ready to roll. When it came to saying Mass, the Monsignor was not one to waste time. With the exception of Nuptial High Masses, which he lingered over theatrically, he whizzed from prayer to prayer like a man stealing base.

"Where's Bad John?" he said, twirling his amice irritably. "If he's not here in two minutes, I guess I'll have to go out there with the likes of you, Kennedy. And don't think I haven't heard you and your Uruguays. Father Sullivan, wherever he is this morning, will just have to say his Mass without a server. And this the last day in Latin to boot. What a way for a language to go!

Whatever became of the virtue of promptness, can anyone tell me that?"

Peanuts found a seat in the corner and folded his hands.

The Monsignor threw him a very hard look, priest to boy, as they listened to Bad John's taps ascend the stairs outside. There was an utter ecclesiastical silence while Bad John slipped out of his tapped loafers and into his rubber-soled Mass-serving shoes.

Peanuts tucked his feet under the chair. Himself, when he served Mass, he'd taken to wearing nonregulation moccasins.

Crepe soles squishing: Peanuts counted six scrambled steps. Bad John was through the door, off balance and breathless.

"Safe!" Monsignor MacMurray spread his arms, vestments and all, in an umpire's stance. "Next time you get here late, Maguire, you're out. *Out*—understand?"

"Yeah, Monsignor." Bad John's cassock, half on, half off, muffled his words. "Sorry, Monsignor."

The door creaked. It was Father Sullivan, making an entrance with his eyes. His cheeks were blurred by an indecisive shave.

"Top of the morning to you, Father," the Monsignor said.

"Good morning to you, Monsignor."

"How are you feeling, Father?" Monsignor MacMurray honk-sniffled.

"Ah, getting old, I guess, Monsignor."

"That's all right, Father. Aren't we all?"

Sullivan took his hands out of his pockets and smiled aimlessly.

The Monsignor nodded to Bad John. They headed for

the altar, cassocks whistling in a mild panic, like roy-
alty who'd lost their police escort.

It took Father Sullivan a while to find a match for his
cigarette. He stood with his back to Peanuts, both
hands on the vestment chest. The wrinkles between his
shoulder blades sank and stretched in time to his shud-
ders. On tiptoe, he reached for something in the cabi-
net. He set it down on the chest with the clear familiar
thud of a shot glass being set on a bar. The back of his
coat rippled again. He poured himself a drink. He
opened the chest and began to lay out his vestments.
He swallowed the rye and poured himself another.

Peanuts, whose mind had lately developed a fond-
ness for precision, registered the time on the wall clock
as thirteen minutes past six. At six-fifteen, he decided,
exactly at a quarter past six, that's when he'd start his
confession. The truth wouldn't take too long.

Father Sullivan, down to his tank shirt, pushed the
shot glass aside. The same shaft of sunlight that was
heating Peanuts' neck struck the glass and set it glowing, a devotional candle.

"What's that, Father?"

His words came freely, without premeditation, but
wondrously planned, like silk from a spider's belly.

Father Sullivan hoisted his glass and smiled.

"That, my boy, is whiskey, as you well know. Here's
to you."

He took a gulp, extended the glass. Peanuts stood up,
the cassock and surplice still over his arm. He took the
glass, shivered at the smell of it. He swallowed.

The second hand swept past six-fifteen.

"Father? . . . Guess what, Father? I broke my ther-
mos." Peanuts shook it; the glass tinkled.

"That's terrible." Father Sullivan drained the whiskey bottle and stuffed his cigarette inside, making a cloud.

"Father?"

"What?"

"The radio said rain today."

Father Sullivan turned to his vestments.

"Do you know how to play chess, Father?"

"I used to."

"I could teach you again, Father."

"Lovely."

"Father, I'd like to make a confession."

"Swell. Wouldn't we all? You're absolutely sure you wouldn't rather just go back to stuttering?"

The chasuble was black with a silver cross, the colors of a commemorative Mass for the dead. The service would be simple and brief. Peanuts, now that he could speak, held no shames about Sister Marian.

"Look kid, it's great you can talk. But I don't want to hear anything I don't want to hear; I don't want to see anything I don't want to see. Find yourself another confessor. The point is, Kennedy, I killed someone."

"Not Sister Marian, Father?"

"No. Sister Marian I did not kill."

"Where is she, Father?"

"Sister Marian is busy." He picked up his chalice. "Don't fret about your sins, Kennedy. There are very few real sins." He polished the lip of the cup with his pinkie. "Just one or two things there's no excuse for."

"Father?"

"What?"

Peanuts knelt down. He had to confess *something*.

"Okay," Father Sullivan said.

"Father, I stole your knife."

"What knife?"

"The switchblade, Father."

"Oh. That's okay, keep it. I traded my overcoat to an Italian guy for it, as I recall."

"I lost it," Peanuts lied. "This morning on the way to church."

"That's good. You could get hurt playing with a thing like that. Is there anything else?"

"No, Father."

Father Sullivan blessed him. Then he, too, knelt down.

"You know, kid, I've often wondered in connection with this job of mine whether I'd let them throttle me first if they were about to burn me at the stake. Would you?"

"Well, Father, one way you'd get to say a few words on your way out and the other way you wouldn't."

Peanuts reached in his belt, handed Father Sullivan the knife and blessed him.

"Lovely." Father Sullivan tossed the knife in the vestment drawer. "Lovely. If there's nothing else, then, professor, let's get on with it, shall we? One last time."

They passed the painting of Saint Cecilia, patron saint of the blind, a martyr, her earthly eyes plucked out as punishment for defending her virtue, the two of them, unusual marbles, on a plate in her left hand. Her other set of eyes, the heavenly ones, installed to symbolize the sight of her soul, rolled up toward the gold rays streaming from the Blessed Trinity, depicted as a pigeon, a bleeding heart and a crown of thorns held in a massive fatherly hand whose wrist was dissolving in a blaze of pure unknowable light.

Peanuts knelt down. Father Sullivan made the sign of the cross.

"Introibo ad altare Dei . . ." he said.

"Ad Deum qui laetificat juventutem meam," Peanuts replied. To God who brings joy to my youth, Uruguay.

At the main altar, off to the right, Monsignor MacMurray was moving right along. The Sisters' soft responses drifted through the vault, snow sweeping the night sea. Sister Marian, of course, was not among them.

At this hour there were only a half-dozen parishioners in the church, listening hopefully to prayers soon to be recited for them. Peanuts knew them all and they all knew him: old people stared at kids voraciously, the way babies stared at everything. Green Gaffney, in full regalia, was snoring, sword across his knees.

Father Sullivan doubled over in a stalled bow and began to shake. He wasn't going to make it.

Peanuts grabbed the plastic card with the prayers on it. On his knees he shifted two steps closer to Father Sullivan. In this position, nobody could see him lifting the priest's hands and pressing them together in the proper pose. Father Sullivan's hands were rough, cold.

Peanuts decided to say the Mass, the priest's dialogue as well as the altar boy's. The priest's lines he read very softly from the card; the altar boy's part he recited briskly.

"Confitebor tibi in cithara, Deus, Deus meus . . ."

"Hold it a second, Kennedy." Father Sullivan was swaying—first his arms, then his whole body. "That's from the psalm of David, which happens to be a love song. So give it a little air. Easy does it, that's the whole idea."

Peanuts, thumping his breast through the *Confiteor*, prayed that all this Latin in one dose would sober his confessor up. Instead, Father Sullivan hunkered down on the altar steps, gathering his chasuble between his knees, and continued to talk in English.

"Free me. Give me a break. First of all, free me from looking up. Then free me from saints. Also free me from your flags and your ascending smells. Free me."

"Et clamor meus ad te veniat!" Peanuts screamed.

Father Sullivan's eyeball broke like a pimple. He took the second bullet above his other eye. The red lightning of the muzzle flash illuminated the front pews, blinding Peanuts, though he saw the gun and the kick of the man's arm away from his crutch. Red thunder.

Peanuts felt, rather than saw, Father Sullivan fly across the altar steps as though he'd been lifted and dropped. When he turned again and faced the gun, there was something he wanted to ask the man for just a moment. There was something he wanted to remember, something he wanted to summon up. And then he understood, as the bullets blew Father Sullivan against the altar, that the man could shoot him too. It would be all right, just a moment, wait please. Wait please. Wait. Thunder.

Cutting Father Sullivan hideously in half, heaving his legs and lower parts much further than the top. Wait. He was the kind of kid who answered knocks on doors. Wait. There was something more to say. Wait.

The man with the vacant sleeve and the gun in his only hand shouted, "I can walk! I'm healed! I can walk!" and threw his crutch away.

He put the gun to his temple. He didn't move until the bullet catapulted his head away, his face a flying red blot, the fragile body streaming after it like a rock on a string.

Peanuts could not get up off his knees. Monsignor MacMurray and Bad John bent in his direction like tall, baffled birds.

The light in the church was dim but not indistinct. Everything was visible, nothing was clear. Certain non-stone things began to bloom like the buds of trees in ancient caves: the mossy green carpeting on the kneeler reserved for visiting bishops, the carved wooden pulpit polished by sermon-pounding hands, and the stained-glass windows splashed with the blood of unimaginable species. The stain was darkening the silver cross on Father Sullivan's chasuble.

Peanuts felt a blow, the impact of a bullet perhaps, punching him like a strong hand, pushing, pushing. He felt wet, helpless; he knew less and less. Cold sweat sucked at his clothes. The panic simplified things, cut his losses. He felt less and less, and there was no room for pain, only voiceless respect for this final feeling. There came a terrible sharp crushing pain in his throat; perhaps he'd been shot there as well. Wet and helpless as at birth, he was becoming altogether light-less, soundless and dreamless until he noticed high on the wall to his right, just between the thirteenth and fourteenth Stations of the Cross, quietly perched, the chill shadow of Uruguay's wingtips touching, waiting for him this one last time.

"RISE."

"Rise," Peanuts repeated. The word—the taste of his life—clicked like a diamond on his tongue. And he heard the horses of the night, their hooves galloping behind the moon.

Peanuts stopped breathing the moment his feet left the floor. The sensation was irresistible, a falling up-

ward: the air was a river becalmed, swollen and slow,
at the mercy of hopes skipped like stones from the
shore.

He rose in sleepless flight, a soaring bird with weight-
less bones. He hovered over the banks of votive candles,
higher than the statue of St. Francis, still tickling his
marble dove, still adored by his deer, and higher into
the darkness, glimpsing the dust on top of the confes-
sional stall, where a spider was strumming her web.
The pews, separating as he rose, were so many straws
strewn in place, and though they were empty, he held
the presence of the parishioners who prayed there;
most of them worked every day but Sunday in stale
shadows. He saw all their futures, but not his own; this
was the only way in which he still felt mortal.

The Band-Aid on his thumb ignited and burned
with a buttercup-colored flame, a tongue of turquoise
at its center. He spread his arms, palms forward. His
knees were slightly bent. His head hung down, resting, resting, drinking from a transparent bowl of
ivory light. The dull silver jets of his tears swooped
to the floor.

He was over the stained-glass windows now, and all
the things in the windows came alive, knowing, vibrating in place, bees suddenly recognizing one another. He
saw everything with sun-bribed eyes: purple serpents,
red ferns, berries of all kinds and colors, wings blue and
gold, scrolls, books, hooks, flutes, lutes, baskets of fruit,
arrows, quivers, towers, faces, he was falling, crosses,
he was falling, hearts bare and bleeding, halos, columns, drinking cups, knotted Celtic vines with no beginnings or ends, he was falling, quill pens, robes,
clasps for robes, executioners' axes, battleaxes, falling,
numbers, words, flowers, birds, loaves of bread, boats,
fishes, crowns . . .

"Okay, Kennedy," Monsignor MacMurray called. "That's enough now. You better get right down here."

. . . pears, caskets, coins, padlocks, clubs, tubs, cliffs, many stars, grapes, moons, castles, turrets, clouds, trombones, fiddles large and small . . .

The clank of Green Gaffney's sword and the sweet stink of incense and gunsmoke, suddenly returning, made him sneeze.

His body shook and the moccasin slipped from his left foot, dropping next to Father Sullivan, whose hand, smeared with blood, still shielded his face.

If Peanuts were dead—and he thought he might have died—he would fall through the floor like a shadow and be swept away by the dark inner bird of death. He imagined in endless swollen colors the nothing he would feel in his final falling seconds. Or would he just stand here in the air till the world swam back again? How long would it take him to sink?

"Come back down here this minute, Kennedy."

Peanuts sneezed, fell. His moccasinless foot recoiled from the floor's marble chill.

Monsignor MacMurray looked at him carefully. "Are you all right now, Dennis?"

Then the Monsignor knelt down to anoint the remains of Father Sullivan's head.

"Let's go," Bad John said. "Baseball's here."

The Brooklyn Botanical Gardens were a mown dream of perfection, Brooklyn died and gone to heaven, fountains soothingly splashing.

Dr. Silberman came for a visit just yesterday. His

new friend Geri, a blonde, bought nine house plants; they had trouble getting them all into the taxi. And Dorothy McDermott stopped by too, the only one of her kids with the courage to find Sister Marian and say good-bye. Dirty Dot, of all people. She was wicked, but she was the best of them.

Today's touring group were all blind children from St. Bridget's. They held hands and made their way through the Scent Garden, fingering the braille plaques that identified every plant.

Marian read the sign they couldn't see:

"F-flowers in this section, boys and girls, are noted for their f-fragrance. Some are even more fragrant in the evening or after a light rain. Scent is important, boys and girls, in attracting insects which pollinate the flowers—the thyme, the savory, the s-spearmint, the apple-scented geraniums . . ."

The children approached a statue fountain: a young woman of brass, all green, naked, a butterfly on her wrist. In front of the fountain, planted in horseshoes, were golden marigolds.

"Please be careful now, boys and girls. Just smell them. They are not to be picked. Only s-smelled."

The children, of course, could not see her crying. Not crying, really. Just a steady flow of tears she couldn't fight, a simple condition which accompanied her speaking about certain plants.

Two of the blind boys strayed among the roses. They amused themselves by brailling the nutty names of experimental hybrids.

"American Home!"

"Snow!"

"Mister Lincoln!"

"Kodachrome!"

"Mamie Eisenhower!"

"Jesuit!"

"Fire Chief!"

"Bob Hope! This one says it's a Bob Hope rose!"

"Hey yeah!" A little girl who'd lost her eyes to lye ran over. "Bob Hope! Mister One-Liner!"

The children all laughed and applauded.

There was a panic. By applauding they'd lost touch with one another. A fluttering of hands; they quickly relinked.

Marian picked the lightest marigold.

"Over here now, boys and girls. Pay attention here. The marigolds smell bitter, like grass. But this one is nearly white. Not perfectly white, of course. Such things are perhaps not possible in this world. This you probably know, you with your special understanding, far better than me with my poor eyes. There is so much unkindness in this world, boys and girls, as we all know. But flowers teach us to pay attention to the beauty. Here, pass it around. This one is one of a kind."

They sniffed and they marveled.

Marian stopped crying.

"And now, boys and girls, right here in Brooklyn, USA—a little bit of the Far East."

They groped toward the Zen Garden, the pond, the pagoda. Marian pinned one of the Bob Hope blooms in her hair, which was short now, almost peeled.

They crossed the wooden bridge, a quiet arch, gently carpentered in the Japanese style.

"Of course," Marian said, "in a Japanese garden there is no center, as you will notice. Our Western gardens, boys and girls, are usually built around a centerpiece. The formal ones, anyway. Watch your steps. In a Japanese garden you have to find your own way,

which should be easy for you, boys and girls. Watch
your steps now. Watch. Some of the stones are very
slippery. Those of you still on the bridge, be careful too.
You wouldn't mistake this for the Brooklyn Bridge,
now would you, boys and girls? That's right, t-touch it."
    "Shhh," somebody said.
    "Que linda!" little Marianita said. She still refused to
speak English.
    "Touch it, boys and girls. That's right. Touch it. Do-
esn't it *feel* like Japan?"

    During lunchtime in the schoolyard, Crazy Doyle
kept mouthing off about the lunatic maniac who'd seen
a miracle in church that morning, the apparition of an
angel it was, and how this nut had pulled a gun and
blew Father Sullivan away, then himself.
    Peanuts was angry at first about this mix-up in mira-
cles, then relieved. He had died and returned to life. It
happened. It was like the Mass. It was the story of a
man who died but didn't. Everybody saw it their own
way. His own miracle, his unique Mass, he consigned
to his head.
    By three in the afternoon the cops had finished their
work. Just half an hour after school let out, the front
doors of Stella Maris had to be locked for the first time
in history. Bad John and Peanuts were the last to
squeeze past Filippo, the janitor, just as he was closing
the side door. They were wearing their baseball uni-
forms. They walked on tiptoes to minimize the clatter
of their spikes on the floor, though this wasn't necessary because the vault was already packed with noise

—not the measured forest sighing of a Mass or Novena, but the pagan babble of hundreds of kids who were filing past the thirteenth and fourteenth Stations of the Cross, where it was reported that the Archangel Michael, greeter of the souls of the dead, had appeared, prophesied, flown and vanished, leaving a stain in the shape of his wings high on the wall. By the time Peanuts got to examine this diversionary angel stain, however, it must have partially dried; there seemed to be the imprint of only one wing.

Filippo walked with them, grinning excitedly.

"You see the stain, man?" he said. "You see the stain? That's nothing, man. You should have seen the priest. They shoot him in the back. Is like my brother Ernesto. They break in his place, they shoot him, they take his pants, his TV, his wallet. Blood all over the place. He in critical condition, man. But not the priest. He finished." Filippo giggled. "I don't think the devil want him up here with us."

Peanuts searched for Uruguay.

The stain was drying before his eyes, shrinking back into the stone.

Peanuts knew. He knew.